# BURN BABY BURN

D.K. Williams

For more information, address:

DKWilliamsLL@yahoo.com

First paperback edition January 2022


ISBN 979-8-9855496-0-7

This book is dedicated to my wonderful husband, Jim, who has always been one of my biggest supporters—no matter how crazy the idea.

Also, a great big thank you, to all of my wonderful friends and family that played a role. Whether you were a beta reader, proof reader or encourager, I couldn't have done this without you. You are forever in my heart.

# BURN BABY BURN

# ONE

From the backseat of the Uber, JW retched vehemently into her large Birkin bag lined with plastic especially for this occasion. The driver glanced into the rear-view mirror upon hearing the blech. As he pulled the car over to the curb, he flinched as the hot stench wafted from the backseat and hit his nostrils.

"God lady, don't get that in my car, shit man, you stink," he said.

"Yeah, I know, but it's our secret," she said.

She popped a breath mint and wiped her mouth with the back of one hand, as she reached for the door handle with the other. JW had arrived, full of dread and late again as usual, she was perpetually late for everything, always.

Leah had even called her two hours earlier to remind her to be in the gallery at 6 PM sharp for a meet and greet with the VIP's. She pled with her not to keep the Upper East Side elite waiting. In addition to tardiness, JW suffered from opening night jitters, and the accompanying anxiety upchucks. A therapist diagnosed her with 'imposter syndrome', and told her it was due to self-doubt, and a fear of exposure as a fraud. She definitely had that fear, and he had no cure. Tonight the syndrome was in full force for the opening of her solo show. This was her third show in as many years at the prestigious NuVeau Eastside Gallery, owned by her best friends Leah and Joseph

Levy.

Leah was afraid too, someday, JW would be a no show for one of her openings. She anxiously peered into the street from the lobby drumming her nails on the champagne flute, wondering if this would be the night. At exactly 6:15, the car pulled up and Leah breathed a sigh of relief. She watched JW's long legs emerge first, then the rest of her wrapped in a pink Louis Vuitton scarf, swirling around her in the wind and catching it in the slamming car door. She jerked it free like it was a worthless old rag, shoved it into her handbag, and took the stairs three at a time to reach the door.

When JW burst into the gallery, everyone noticed and there was an audible gasp, as if anticipating her arrival without expecting it.

Clad in all black cashmere, the sweater dress hugged her svelte body and her straight blonde hair hung with a precision cut framing her flawless porcelain face. A large hammered silver amulet hung around her neck like a medal of honor. She was breathtaking to look at but truly did not realize it.

JW was one of those beauties that people notice, when they glide into the room, she seemed to float rather than walk. Standing at over six feet tall, and after all of her 35 years, she was accustomed to stares by now, but still not comfortable with it. Always a gangly girl, JW believed people stared because she was a foot taller than her peers were. She always felt awkward and never belonged, anywhere. Then one day she realized she was right, she did not.

As a child she could hardly wait to escape the small Kentucky backwoods town fate dropped her into like a sack of unwanted kittens. In order to cope with her misfit life, she had always carried pencil and paper in her hand sketching or doodling something. Many times, she drew images on the brown paper bags that carried home their meager food stamp allotment. Her art became her best and only friend, and then a passion, and then she found she soared with it. Her imaginations never laughed at her hand-me-downs with too short sleeves and high water pants, and dirty Dollar Store canvas shoes with holes in the toes. Her art was never judgmental toward her, and so far, in life, it had not abandoned her.

From her sorrowful childhood, she had transformed into a unique and classic woman, and she never wore flats to compensate for those vertically challenged around her. Comfortable in 3" heels, towering over people had become her norm. She did not seem to realize how intimidating she was, especially to men, nor did she care—not anymore.

Once JW was inside the gallery Leah rushed toward her, handing her a bubbling flute of Cristal, and taking her by the elbow. Leah was adept at handling JW with all her insecurities. She guided her toward the largest and most expensive piece she had hanging in the gallery, all in one smooth move. There was a small group of very wealthy collectors standing elbow-to-elbow around the latest massive work. They were trying to impress each other with their descriptions of the subtle meaning of brush strokes, brilliant use of color values and intricate patterns that danced upon the canvas.

Leah estimated packing the gallery tonight with over 300 patrons to the invitation only event, which she thought was a stellar turnout. Now, if only these art lovers brought their Amex Black Cards with them tonight, and used them.

The Gallery had once been an old warehouse, Joseph and Leah bought as an investment property fifteen years ago, and was now prime real estate on the upper Manhattan East Side. The exterior facade was old red brick with white limestone trim around the double doors and the large storefront windows. Joseph had renovated the inside into a modern industrial showcase, with lots of white walls, recessed lighting, black ironwork, and painted the ceiling matte black. Large industrial ceiling fans rotated in a slow turn, black metal piping served as handles on the tall doors. State of the art lighting, which automatically dimmed or brightened, depending upon time of day or night, illuminated the art for optimal viewing, ambient lighting was installed to enhance skin tones—no fluorescent lighting was allowed anywhere in the gallery. Everything was opulent, no expense spared in the redesign. Custom windows faced the street to display the large art pieces hanging on the main wall, so people walking down the sidewalk could see the images. The layout allowed patrons walking in the front door to smack into an immense display wall of JW's art. There were well over 100 pieces hanging tonight, ranging in price from $1500 to $500K dollars.

In the design process, Joseph wanted to

accommodate a workspace and inventory storage area as well. To do so, he walled off the center of the building, to house a large open studio, with skylights providing natural light. JW installed a mini kitchen, bath, and cot so when she felt inspiration for a major project or series, she wouldn't need to go to her apartment. She would work without stopping, crash, wake, work, eat, sleep, and repeat.

For tonight's gala, while soothing classical music played in the background through an expensive sound system, wait staff dressed in black circulated to serve hors d'oeuvres and champagne in Waterford flutes. On the menu was vegan queso dip, made with pureed cashews flavored with spices like cayenne pepper and cumin, a sumac hummus made with herbs and served with pita chips, and oven-dried savory and spicy sliced tofu jerky strips. For the pescatarians, a mini smoked salmon pizza—a small baked crostini bread with a dab of cream cheese and a small piece of smoked salmon with dill and capers on top.

Leah pinged her ring against the glass to garner everyone's attention. "Everyone, here she is—JW DuValle. The featured artist of tonight's solo event that recently accomplished a $1M sale at Sotheby's for her acclaimed piece, 'Into the Night'." She waved her arm toward JW to direct all eyes on her. There was a round of applause, and JW tried not to blush as she slightly bowed at the waist.

Leah was not only a good friend but she was an excellent art dealer/broker. She was shrewd with passion and possessed great knowledge of the art market. A consummate professional, she knew JW's art was wildly collectible, and would only increase in value. She learned that just this week Christie's auction house sold digital art by Beeple for $69M. Proving once again, rich people would buy good art, and there were a lot of them in this room tonight.

She and Joseph had supported and promoted JW since their first art class together at NYU, which seemed like an eternity ago. They shared a mutual admiration and great friendship. They loved her work ethic and character, she admired their love for one another and their families, and it didn't hurt that together they had made a lot of money for all of them.

After the introduction, JW extended her manicured hand to the group and began her evening performance.

Not long into the evening charade, JW heard her cell phone ring and since the only two people that would call her were in this room, she felt compelled to answer. While digging in the massive purse without dislodging the bag of vomit, a strange foreboding overcame her. She excused herself, stealing away from the group to answer the call.

"Hi, is this JW DuValle, or should I call you Wanda Jane Walker? This is Shore and Shore Law Firm in Leitchfield, KY," without waiting for an answer he continued, "Your Aunt Minnie has named you as a beneficiary in her last will and testament."

Without taking a breath, the man went on, "Can't believe I found you…....…."

The last words she heard were 'I found you', the

rest were mushed together and nonsensical. Her mind started racing, and she couldn't catch her breath. A full-blown panic attack ensued as beads of sweat formed on her upper lip. Her vision started to shrink into tiny black pinpoints. The room started to spin. Just like Alice falling down the rabbit hole, she went down.

Her head was in Joseph's lap and Leah was lightly smacking her face when she roused and she was so embarrassed. After reinventing herself, changing her name, and all the years of hiding, her past found her today. She naively believed that when she had escaped that two-bit town, she would be free from all her ghosts. Her wild eyes betrayed her. If the people in this room found out who she really was it would ruin her. JW was born someone else, another name, another life, and thought she had made it out of that nightmare—that she had escaped completely. Alas, she did not.

"All you need to do is get through tonight, just breathe," Leah said.

Leah had been her best friend since they were college roommates over 18 years ago. She knew how broken JW was then and remained today. JW thought that after all these years, the trauma would lessen to some degree. Her philosophy was to pretend it didn't happen, and it will go away. However, what she found out was you can't push your past deep inside and ignore it, that only makes it come out in some other form as something else. She was a perfect example: imposter syndrome, vomiting in your handbag, anorexia, or never trusting anyone to love you because in the end, they all leave you. She was conditioned to believe all you have is yourself in life, and it's better that way. Do not set yourself up for more disappointment. The only other person she ever let get close was Leah, and she had been there for her so far, but she probably had a limit too. She thought, for in the end they all leave, don't they?

# TWO

JW looked out the airplane window to survey the Kentucky bluegrass and manicured horse farms below, and when she thought about returning to her birthplace it made her stomach queasy. Not much of the surroundings seemed to have changed since she left on the Greyhound bus headed north to a new life, but she certainly had. When she boarded the bus fresh out of high school, she was a different person, she also answered to a different name—Wanda Jane. That name would never suit her new life, so she had changed it—just like that, she became JW when she disembarked that Greyhound in New York City.

Now 18 years later, she was returning to Kentucky, and she reflected on her pitiful childhood. Getting away had not been easy, nothing in her life had ever been easy. Only one thing was still missing, she had always wanted a family, her own to give and get love, and someone who would care about her and stick around. She never had that as a child. She had been the caregiver, the mother, everything to everyone. The only family she had now was by mutual adoption, a friend like a sister. That was her Leah. Her mind went back to the beginning of her escape from hell and it all began with a seat on a Greyhound bus when she was 17.

She had worked hard to earn her seat on that bus, she saved every nickel, and dime she could find, finished school with a 3.8 GPA, scored a 1400 on her SATs, applied for every Pell Grant, scholarship and loan she could find while taking care of Momma.

Finally, she escaped and was terrified. She sat on that bus shaking like a scared bunny, while clutching her life savings with white knuckled fist, and exactly $279.18 in her jacket pocket. She knew down to the penny, as she had counted it repeatedly. It had been an almost insurmountable task for her to collect and save that much cash. That money and the small cloth sack she toted, and the clothes on her back were all she had to her fictitious new name.

In order to transport herself to a new life in New York City, she began saving her lunch money instead of spending the .35 cents that her Momma had given her each morning. Even that eventually stopped because Momma found her change purse completely empty near the end of the month. Sometimes for lunch, she would splurge and eat a chocolate covered cherry cone in the school cafeteria, and then she felt guilty. It would usually make her sick to her stomach to have this sweet when it mixed with the bile acid in her hollow belly. To try to earn more money, she also babysat for the orneriest kids in the county; four boys aged six to ten. Every Thursday night she walked over a mile to their tiny pink house, while the parents bowled in the gravel pit coed league at the Rainbow Lanes bowling alley. She fed the boys dinner, oversaw baths, teeth brushing and a raucous bedtime ritual repeated at least five times for it to stick. For these four hours of weekly punishment, she made the heady sum of $4, and then she walked herself home alone in the dark. By the end of her senior year, she vowed to never birth children, and she was a walking skeleton, tipping the scale at 113 lbs., on a six-foot frame. All the popular girls at school looked at her with envy, as they counted calories and exercised to maintain a perfect size eight. The lack of nutrition dulled her skin and dark circles appeared under sallow eyes. Her hair was dry and brittle so she brushed it back into a ponytail, skillfully covering what she thought were too large ears. One thing Wanda Jane always wore though was a smile plastered on her face for Momma. She certainly had nothing to smile about, it was the only other lie she ever told.

As she neared graduation day, she said, "Momma, I need to tell you somethin, an you're a not gonna like it. After I graduate high school this May, I 'ma be goin' to art school in New York City. Miss Jenkins, the guidance counselor at school has been helpin me."

Momma's eyes grew wider and teared up, "You're gonna leave me? But, what will I do?"

Wanda Jane rushed on while she still had courage, "Momma, I got a scholarship, and applied for somethin' called 'FAFSA' and Pell Grants, and I can get a part-time job at the school, and I've been savin' all summer....", as her voice trailed off, Momma winced and raised her hand in protest. Wanda Jane clasped it gently lowering it to her lap, as she said, "Momma, I'm goin...ain't nothin stoppin' me, not even you."

While preparing to leave for school in the fall,

Wanda Jane had to find a place for Momma. This worried her every day, and try as she mite she was at a loss for an answer.

It fell to her, as the only child in the marriage between Sarah Jane and Samuel Walker to be Momma's caretaker. Daddy had been a hard worker until the day he died. That happened the year she turned eight, one day right there in the middle of the new Walmart in aisle 6, Daddy dropped deader than a doornail. He went there between his day shift job and his night shift job, to buy a six-pack of Mt. Dew—his drink of choice and the only vice that she knew about. Daddy was an absentee parent before anyone knew what that meant. He was always working to pay the rent, the doctor bills and for Momma's medicine. Wanda Jane wasn't surprised when he left them, she guessed he just couldn't take it anymore and took the easy way out. Everybody leaves, don't they?

As long as Wanda Jane could remember, arthritis crippled Momma. Her hands were swollen, misshapen, and drawn into claws that always reminded Wanda Jane of swan's wings. Purple spots of blood blisters covered her arms up to her shoulders, so Momma always wore long sleeves. Her knees were twice the size of a normal person, and her feet and ankles where frozen stiff from joint damage. But, Momma always had the best smile for Wanda Jane. Around Momma, Wanda Jane was a born comedian; she could make Momma laugh more than anybody could. That is what she remembered best about her Momma.

There were many scary memories too. Like the time Momma accidently bumped her shin on the bed footboard, her skin was so fragile that she and ended up in six hours of surgery, a three-day hospital stay, with six weeks of bandage changes with a permanent chunk of her leg missing. The doctor said the thin skin was from the cortisone shots she got weekly to calm the inflammation and tolerate the constant pain. One-time she accompanied Momma to the doctor, she watched as old Doc Jones jabbed needles into each knee and drained a couple of syringes of greenish/yellow fluid, he then shot in cortisone, gave her another dose in the hip and sent her home, with daily pain pills. That was the only time Wanda Jane went in with Momma. She couldn't stand to watch.

In addition to skin breakdown, the medicine caused her face to balloon into a moon shape, and brought erratic mood swings. Wanda Jane never knew if Momma would greet her with tears, anger, or be one of the few days, she would lay in bed with the curtains drawn all day, on those days she could hear her softly crying. Wanda Jane never blamed her and Momma suffered enough without adding to her sorry lot. But one thing Wanda Jane could count on, Momma would never give in to the disease and quit trying—quit walking, quit living. She refused a wheel chair and couldn't afford a fancy lift chair, to stand up she would rock the old and cracked Naugahyde recliner three or four times until it spit her up onto her feet. She would stand there teetering like a toddler just learning to walk until she found sure footing, and then carefully and slowly start inching forward.

As crippled as Momma was, she still did her best to mother a now fatherless Wanda Jane. Wanda Jane's favorite thing—until she was nine was to gingerly lay across Momma's lap in the big old recliner, pull up her shirt exposing her bony back. Momma would then drag her claws around in swirls to tickle, scratch, rub, and pat until she was soothed, sometimes for hours if needed. All that would fade into a precious memory.

The summer Daddy died, Wanda Jane remembered sitting on the front porch step with her baby doll, as the cold concrete seeped deep into her bones. It found the hollowness inside her tiny body and made itself at home.

She cuddled a plastic baby doll. The baby had seen better days with its face hand-tatted with blue ballpoint ink. The previous owner embellished her eyebrows and lips with blue ink to try to bring them back to life. Her hair had been hacked at with scissors, and lots of plastic scalp with holes that once held synthetic hair showed through. Washed and dried matted clumps of fuzz were all that remained on her poor head. Someone donated the doll in a box of hand-me-downs at the school for the poor kids. The doll clothes once belonged to her, Momma had pulled out of a box in the closet. She swaddled her baby in a ratty old bleached out receiving blanket. Nevertheless, she loved her plastic tatted-up baby, she would hold her and rock her and sing made-up songs as she wished someone would sing to her.

Their concrete porch slab had pieces broken away

as if it had been a war zone at one time, but its only curse was being in a poverty zone. Paint peeled and curled hanging onto the front of the old rental house and one of her solitary past times was pulling and collecting paint chips.

The screen door had a hole where someone's hand had pushed one to many times, and flies seemed to know where to breech for entry. The yard had a patch of dirt that began at the left side of the house and arced outward like half a moon. This patch of dirt was one of her favorite play areas, it was soft dusty red clay that she could dig holes and push small cars through the make believe roads. When she tired of the cars, she would draw a large circle and shoot marbles in the ring in the dirt, things lonely children did to occupy their days.

Today had been amazing for she saw other kids, and maybe they would want to play with her. The dilapidated house next door had new neighbors moving in and she had been watching the comings and goings of the pickup truck with her wide, dark circled and sad eyes. The truck had made two or three trips offloading loads of furniture and a few cardboard boxes. Then the kids started arriving and running around the house looking for new adventures. She counted six of them. There were three boys and three girls and some of the kids looked to be about her age too.

There had once been an attempt at a wire fence between her house and the new neighbor's house, but not much of it remained upright. What was there now was grownup with grass and weeds, and the kids began trying to climb on it right away. She also saw they had a dog. It was a mangy looking, skinny thing, but it followed the kids everywhere around the yard. She always wanted a dog, but Momma said no.

She was in awe of the activity next door, as an only child, she had never experienced such commotion and loudness. The Roller family had arrived, and everyone knew it by the sounds they emitted. These kids knew how to play too. The boys had sticks that became swords, and fingers that became guns for a hearty game of 'cops 'n robbers', the girls played school a lot and the mother was always finding things for them to do. Magically large cardboard refrigerator boxes would appear, and these would become houses or lemonade stands until the kids destroyed it.

It wasn't long before Wanda Jane joined in the raucous fun. In the hot summer nights before the lighting bugs would arrive, they'd play a game of kick-the-can. All you needed to play this game was an old used tin can and the ability to run. In July, they would capture June bugs, tie a piece of thread to its leg, and race them around and around the yard until tired of them, and then they'd release them. The creek in the woods behind the house was teaming with tadpoles, frogs, and crawdads and a favorite spot on hot days. Anything they could find to play with was fair game. The kids played softball, kickball, red-rover, Simon says, and rolling down grassy hills. One day the Roller's got a shiny new swing set for their backyard, it didn't last long, but it was a beauty when it first arrived. It had two swings, and a glider that had a bench on each side for perpetual motion, a shiny metal slide, and a chin-up bar for acrobatics. The swing set had a problem, if you got too high, one of the legs would pull up off the ground and threaten to flip the entire set over. It was for dare devil use only. Also, the shiny metal slide sitting in the hot sun would scorch any bare skin exposed to it.

The best thing that happened that summer was that Lucy Roller became her friend. She was a roly-poly sickly girl. Lucy's mother would not let her play outside if her hair was wet or if she coughed, but when she could play she was her favorite. They played dress up with some old long gowns Mrs. Roller found one day, their house was awesome, things would just show up for them to play with. Usually if she was around at mealtime, she would just get in line and be fed with the rest of the kids, nobody noticed or cared.

It soon became apparent that Mr. Roller had a problem. He would come home from work in the evening and start drinking, and you could palpably feel the atmosphere change. Kids would hide, become quiet, always be outside, and even sometimes come over to her house to escape. Then they would hear the Roller's fighting, yelling, crying, slapping, and more crying and then the eerie silence. The kids would stay outside or at Wanda's house, for as long as they could before they had to go home. One day Lucy told her that her daddy had a special bottle. When he drank from it, her dad went away, and in his place, a monster would come. She did not understand that for a long time, but as she got older, she did.

That fall the Roller family moved away as quickly as they had arrived, and Wanda Jane was once again on her own. Wanda Jane learned many valuable lessons that summer: that everybody has a demon of some sort, and they just shapeshift depending upon the circumstance. She learned about getting, she learned how to blend into the crowd to survive, how to hide from trouble, and how not to love anyone, because they all end up leaving in the end.

As bad as that eighth summer was losing daddy and her only friend, her ninth would be far worse and she would lose so much more. It would steal more from her. It would rob her sense of innocence, her safety, her laughter, and her hope. Wanda Jane would not let anyone ever touch her again after that ninth summer. It changed her life forever, and would always be her dirty, nasty, well-kept secret.

Nevertheless, she continued to grow and plot her escape from 'hell Ville', as she called it. When she was 17, with graduation looming and on the cusp of her disappearing, she worried about what would happen to Momma. The answer to that problem seemed to come out of nowhere, Aunt Minnie showed up just in time for once in her life.

# THREE

Momma always told her that her Aunt Minnie was the meanest woman in Grayson County, and often said, "she was too mean to die'. She wondered why Momma said this until the day they went to visit her one summer day when she was four years old. Afterward, she agreed.

On this particular Sunday in June, Daddy drove the old green '70 Chevy flare side pickup truck, with the stick shift on the column, carrying Wanda and Momma to the old family farm now the home of Aunt Minnie. They pulled the truck, onto the steep hillside driveway in front of the farmhouse. Out of the truck windshield, in the front yard she saw Aunt Minnie raise a hatchet high in the air, her wiry gray and white fuzzy hair blowing around her head like a wild cat. Her large dark glasses had slid and rested halfway down her long sweaty nose, which strangely looked just like her Momma's. With one hand raising the ax, the other held the scraggly legs of a rooster laying across an old stump. It squawked as if it knew what was coming for its scrawny neck. As the hatchet in her hand started its downward decent, Wanda covered her eyes and let out a wail. The head went one way and the body the other. She turned the rooster loose, and it flopped and ran around the yard—without its head, it was the strangest sight she had ever seen.

Without missing a beat Aunt Minnie said, "You're just in time for supper; it'll be ready in about an hour or so."

From that day forward, Wanda was scared to death of that mean ole woman; but she did make great fried chicken and biscuits. Wanda was still too young to realize that her dinner that day was the headless dancing chicken running around the yard an hour before.

Aunt Minnie was Momma's oldest sister and only remaining relative. The girls, raised in a strict home, by a fire and brimstone circuit preacher and his submissive wife, were born one year apart. There had been another girl birthed to the couple, her name was Sarah, but she had died at the age of two. Momma remembered the day she died. Suddenly one day the youngest baby took sick with fever and then broke out in hives from head to toe, started gasping for air, and then her lips started turning blue. Her daddy was not home with the truck, and her Momma had no telephone, no help—just three babies.

Aunt Minnie ran all the way to the nearest neighbor, which was about three miles down the rutted clay orange dirt road. However, by the time help arrived the baby was gone to heaven, Momma said. They believed the hives went inward and Sarah choked to death.

They wrapped her in a light pink blanket and buried her in the back yard, with nothing but a rock for proof that she had once lived. Momma heard her Daddy hammering out in the barn most of the night. He was making a little coffin out there with leftover boards he had used to build a chicken coop. Her mother lay the baby to rest on a feather pillow that she had covered with her most beautiful embroidered pillowcase. The white one with tiny blue flowers, and the hand crocheted white lace around the edge. She still remembered when Momma told this story as she fingered the edge of her skirt, as if she was touching the pillowcase that embraced her baby sister for eternity. No one ever really knew why this happened to the baby.

Her Daddy pastored two churches and as a circuit preacher, each Sunday he would rotate between congregations. He barely made enough money to buy them a single jersey milk cow, they had a few chickens for eggs and meat, and they planted a small garden and canned what they harvested. They didn't starve; they survived, but just barely.

When the girls were teenagers they did what most young preacher's kids in the poor south did in those days, they rebelled. They discovered boys, smoking, drinking, running wild, and found their escape route. The girls married young, submitting to their husbands as trained, had babies, and prepared to start the cycle of poverty all over again.

As long as Wanda could remember, Aunt Minnie was a widow. She once heard Momma talking about the husband that had died before Wanda had memory. Evidently, this was the second one. The official story was that he was walking home from town, with a 'snoot' full of liquor and had fallen off the 14 mile creek bridge bashing in his head, or so that's the story that was told. Momma and Daddy also whispered about Aunt Minnie's uncanny aim and ability to use a cast iron skillet with deadly consequences.

The first husband, whose name was never spoken aloud, was also the sire of a doubly scary and no account cousin—Luther. It seems dear old hatchet wielding, cast-iron swinging Auntie Minnie had been a bad judge of men, and then she went and spawned one too. What bad luck. Judging from unnamed, Uncle #1's offspring, said uncle had been nothing to write home about, and Momma never told how he met his untimely demise. Wanda knew he existed, for one day while exploring the farm, she found an unkempt grave, with a small hand carved stone under a big tree behind the farmhouse. It looked as if someone had thrown away a flat rock into a pile of brush. She stubbed her toe on it as she was running away from or to something.

In the end though, Aunt Minnie did come through for her and Momma the year she needed her to make her escape. Wanda could never expect any other help from her though. When Wanda left for college, Aunt Minnie let Momma move into the farmhouse with her. At the time, Cousin Luther was getting free lodging in the Eddyville State Prison, called the 'Castle on the Cumberland'. It was a super max prison for the worst offenders in the penal system. Locked up for many years in the smaller county jails for petty crimes, now Luther had finally graduated to a State Penitentiary. His sentence to Eddyville was 30 years for attempted murder of some poor soul that had the misfortune to cross his path.

Luther was a completely new level of mean, even as a boy. He was seven years older than Wanda Jane was, and as her only family, they would visit the farm quite often. One summer memory was when she turned seven, she went to see the barn cat's new litter of kittens, but Luther had beat her to them. She heard before she saw his handiwork. The mother cat was distressed and meowing loudly for her babies. When she approached the wide-open barn door, Wanda Jane saw pure evil looking at her with a smile on his dark face. He had a scar that ran from an inch above his left eyebrow to his cheek. It was evident that somebody had done a poor job of stitching him up at some point.

"Did ya come ta see the widdle kitties? Well they been hangin' around for ya." he sneered and cackled as he stepped away, opening her view into the barn.

She saw the poor babies hanging from a rafter with a grass string from a hay bale around each tiny stretched neck. They had already grown stiff, and were swinging in the breeze. Their tongues were hanging out of their open mouths, the life gone out of them, and their eyes had not even opened from birth yet. She was terrified and let out a blood-curdling scream and then bolted. She ran and ran and ran, and knew then that he would do anything to anybody and she made it a practice to stay far away from Luther. However, as fate would have it, far away was not far enough.

The good news was that Luther's all-expense paid trip to Eddyville all these years later, had freed up a spare room at Aunt Minnie's for Momma. They both needed the company, but Aunt Minnie still charged Momma rent for room and board—kind hearted Aunt Minnie. Aunt Minnie did take Momma to her weekly doctor's appointments and took care of her while she was dying and for that, Wanda was grateful.

After the news from home about Momma's death, she lost touch with anyone in Grayson County. There was no funeral for Momma. Wanda had no money for a bus ticket home, so it just was another heartbreak to suffer in silence. Someone else in life had left her, so she did what she always did, she turned to her art, buried the hurt deep inside and ran away again.

No one ever contacted or tried to find her again. She sure as hell did not make it easy for them to do so, good riddance.

# FOUR

When JW got off that bus in New York City, she finally caught a lucky break. She got Leah Wasserman as a college roommate, and then Leah got Joseph Levy as a husband and JW finally got a family.

Leah Wasserman and JW were roommates at the Weinstein Hall freshman dormitory at Tisch School of Arts, NYU. Leah was the quintessential virtuous Jewess, whose family lived in Manhattan. The girls shared more than a dorm room; each had a mutual love of art and worked hard to be successful. Leah was as homely as she was rich, she had tons of dark curly hair and a Romanesque nose, but none of that mattered to JW. JW soon found herself traipsing home with Leah to celebrate Shabbat every Friday night beginning at sundown with the Wasserman family. This was how she first learned to navigate so well the social waters outside of one culture while faking it into another, and she would learn to master that skill.

JW realized after arriving at Tisch, that her southern drawl was a huge detriment in the art community where she desired to become a charter member. Upon hearing her utter a word, hardened New Yorker's would immediately discredit her intelligence and fellow artist perceived her as a hayseed without talent or credentials. So, each evening when the ABC World News Tonight came on with Diane Sawyer as anchor, who also happened to be a Kentucky native, JW tuned in and practiced her diction. Nightly, she would repeat Diane's spiel, mimic the mouth shapes, and practice delivering the ten-dollar words, as Momma used to call them. By the end of her first year, she commanded a weird dialect that landed somewhere between upper Manhattan socialite and a bubeleh.

Next, she needed to address her style. Clearly, the sack of clothes from the Dollar Store and Goodwill did not fit in at Tisch. However, since this school was so eclectic her style didn't need much work. Tischies revel in their quirkiness, many of the up and coming artist regularly shop at local thrift stores, not of need but of want. JW made a few solo trips to the local thrift stores, and nabbed some cast-offs that Leah was going to donate anyway and she was all set.

Neither of the young women had come to college with friends, didn't make friends, and the sorority sisters did not attempt to recruit them during rush week. As oddballs, they fit in so well and quickly became official "Tischie's," at the college known for its "gypsies, tramps, and white collar thieves." Unbeknownst when she applied but later learned on her arrival, this is the same college and same dormitory hall that birthed Def Jam Recordings in 1984, in the dorm room of student Rick Rubin, while using Tisch recording equipment. Shortly afterwards Russell Simmons joined the label and the rest of the story is R&B, Punk Rock and Rap legend history. She was proud of that fact.

So together the two young women fell into an

easy rhythm of college life, where neither of them belonged as usual. Only this time they were with likeminded artist, and they found their tribe. Leah was also understanding of JW's insomnia and night terrors. The first week of screams in the middle of a peaceful night was difficult and frightened Leah. But, she would always rush to her new friend and sit with her, make her chamomile tea to soothe her and just 'be'. She learned early on not to touch her, or hug her after a night terror. In time, the frightful nights seemed to diminish in intensity, but JW never dated or let anyone get close to her.

The only fly in the ointment, as far as JW was concerned, was that Leah met Joseph during her senior year, with the help of a "shadchan"—a matchmaker that Mother Wasserman knew.

Mother Wasserman decided it was time for Leah to attend a "bashow." Known as a sit in, or chaperoned quasi-date. Joseph and his parents came to visit Leah at the Wasserman home to see if they might be compatible. This is the only time that JW remembered she was not welcomed to attend a Wasserman family affair. She was to remain sequestered upstairs in Leah's bedroom for the evening. However, she did manage to sneak to the bannister and listen to what transpired in the rooms below. Much of the conversation slid fluently in and out of Yiddish and Hebrew, and even though she had been trying to learn the language for three years with Leah as a patient teacher, she was, after all, a gentile from Kentucky.

At their first meeting, it was apparent to the

Wasserman and Levy parents that the matchmaker, was heavenly ordained and the two had found their other half on the first try. Joseph was Leah's 'basheter'—her destiny, her soulmate. Like all new love stories, they soon became inseparable.

Joseph and Leah were betrothed within a month, and upon receiving her engagement ring, she and Joseph were given a slip of paper with a telephone number and PIN by the Dor Yeshorim, which provides genetic screening to young adults. After betrothal, a couple would take a blood test, and later dial the special phone number and enter their PINs. This genetic testing center would tell them if their union was safe to have healthy children. Joseph and Leah were going to be married, they just were not sure if they should have children. The days leading up to the results of the PIN reveal were stressful, and JW would often see Leah crying and in great anguish.

Leah said, "what if we can't have children? What man wants to marry a barren woman?"

JW felt so sorry for her friend. One day JW observed Leah crying again, she went to her friend and said, "Leah, I know this is so difficult, and I don't have all the answers. But, seems to me, if God has ordained you two to be together, don't you think the final say belongs to Him, not a piece of paper?"

Leah grabbed JW, and hugged her so tightly and said from this day forward you are my 'Shvester' (sister); you are family, 'Mishpokhe'.

Leah and Joseph never dialed the number; they didn't care what the genetic testing revealed, because they were meant to be together. They threw the PIN numbers in the trash. They were married a year later and Joseph became the man that wanted to grant Leah's every desire, which he did, and JW finally found her family.

# FIVE

The plane landing on the runway jarred her out of the past and brought her back to the sad reality. She always felt this way after she thought of her childhood, she wished that wasn't so. All she wanted to do now was to drive to Leitchfield, get this business over with, and get out of town as quickly as possible.

Now here she was returning to the one place she hoped never to lay eyes on again in her lifetime. For the hasty trip to Kentucky, JW reserved a flight, but no hotel. She planned to rent a car at the airport and find a room after the hour drive to Leitchfield. Surely, in the 18 years since she had left, there had been a hotel or two built nearby. Especially since, they were so close to tourist attractions like the Mammoth Cave National Park, and beautiful lakes that dotted the region.

"Hey Leah, I wanted to let you know I've arrived safely. This should be a quick trip; I hope to have this stuff wrapped up and back in a week." She said in the voice mail.

It was as if rote memory took over and she wheeled the car out of the airport parking lot heading southbound on I65, without even looking at the GPS. A gorgeous June day she put the windows down and let the sweet smell of country air rush into her nostrils. A good memory flooded her mind; her life here had not been all-bad. She recalled a hot and humid summer afternoon laying on a creek bank at the farm with her feet dangling in the cold spring rushing down from the mountain. While catching tadpoles and saving them in mason jars til they sprouted legs and lost tails, becoming frogs.

Her revelry was broken when she spied the Elizabethtown exit from I65. She circled the town courthouse square once, which circled the three-story brick building like a wheel with spokes. Not bothering to take any road that shot off the roundabout, she pulled into a parking space reaching for her cell phone. There was a new motel in the town, which she found was fully booked. The clerk was kind enough to recommend a local B&B run by the Cooper Family Farm, a chirpy voice answered on the first ring.

"Hello, this Katie, at the Cooper Family Farm B&B, how can I help you?"

JW smiled and said to herself, "You're not in Kansas anymore Dorothy." No one in New York was that nice on the telephone.

"Hi, I need a room for a few days, starting today, any chance?"

"This must be your lucky day," Katie said. "We just had a cancellation and I have a queen with private bath open. It goes for $89 a night, plus tax."

Without hesitation, JW quickly said, "I'll take it."

She found the B&B easy enough. When she pulled into the gravel driveway, something about

31

the Victorian house looked vaguely familiar, but she couldn't quite put her finger on it. The Cooper farm was everything you would expect a B&B in the South to look like in the heady summer months. The front porch was expansive; the gray painted floorboards harbored matching crisply painted white wicker rockers with red cushions. The Boston ferns were full and green and hanging evenly spaced around the porch. In the flower bed there was a wrought iron shepherd's hook suspending a hummingbird feeder and the tiny birds were jousting each other in a battle for nectar. She heard the mooing cows in the fields dotted with round bales of freshly rolled hay. She breathed it all in deeply.

The country smells, oh, she had forgotten what that was like. This aroma was one of the things she had missed most about leaving, other than Momma. She discovered in New York that city had a smell of its own, aging sour trash from the dumpsters, sewer water from the gutters, and burnt exhaust fumes. She could never breathe deeply there.

The landscaping around the house was beautiful too. Five-foot tall blue hydrangea stems with broad deep green leaves and clustered blooms the size of small cantaloupes that draped majestically around the foundation. They were interspersed with rich blue-green hosta's and striped lariope tucked in neatly, at just the right places. Running beside the creek rock walkway to the entrance, she admired the ground hugging soft wooly lamb's ear spread invasively along the rocks with tall blooming purple lavender bordering the path. She let her fingertips trail along the purple hued beauties and dislodged the scent into the air. She stopped and took a deeper breath. Glancing over her shoulder as she approached the front door, she took in the view that looked upon rolling acres of green between the white spindles surrounding the porch and the gingerbread trim on each side of the porch columns. Maybe, she thought, this won't be so bad after all.

Inside, as she rang the bell, a pleasant twenty-something young woman appeared and said, "Hey, you must be JW?"

"Right you are." She said.

As Katie, she assumed, was finalizing the paperwork the backdoor opened and slammed shut, and in walked a familiar and good-looking face. JW tried not to stare and appear nonchalant, but she was sure she had seen those eyes and the handsome man before. He was her height, short-cropped light brown hair—with just the right amount of gel lifting the front hairline where it was naturally hi-lighted by the sun. His face and arms revealed a deep brown farmer's tan, accentuated by a white T-shirt, which showed his chest muscles and the bulge of his large biceps. She couldn't help but notice the tight blue jeans and cowboy boots. In his hand, he held a well-worn cowboy hat, which he tossed expertly onto the hat hook on the wall. She hoped she did not gasp audibly when she saw him.

Without missing a beat, he approached her and said, "Wanda Jane, I'd know you anywhere, how have you been? My gosh, I haven't seen you since graduation day." Not waiting for a response or recognition, he reached for her hand and wrapped both of his around hers and said, "You are as beautiful as ever," as he leaned in to kiss her cheek. She drew slightly away, but not before she smelled him, mixtures of sweet tobacco snuff, fresh sweat and a whiff of

cologne. She closed her eyes and enjoyed the moment.

Then panic struck her, her hands began to tremble slightly, as she wrenched free. Her eyes darted around to find the nearest exit and then she stammered, "I'm-I'm terribly sorry, but I can't seem to place you?"

He said, "It's me, Charlie, Charlie Cooper, we graduated together, remember. Granted, I have filled out a bit since the scrawny kid in class, but I would know you anywhere. You are prettier than you were in high school, and that's hard to believe."

Now she remembered, and she could feel the heat rise up from her neck to her face. She knew he saw her flush, but he never let on. Suddenly she had a vision of 8th grade, 2nd period Algebra class, Mr. Doss. A group of boys in the back of the class all snickering as she entered, she assumed about her. It was a day, she happened to wear one of the two dresses she owned. Usually, it was an old pair of holey jeans, before they were in style, or a pair of hand-made blue pants with strawberry designs, or one of the dresses, and that was the entirety of her school wardrobe that year. Well, this memorable day as she was about to sit down prior to class starting, one of the boys quickly pulled her chair out from under her and splat, down she went. The dress went up, and a pain like one she had never felt before shot up from her tailbone. Everyone was staring at her as she screamed, all she could do was scramble to her feet and run to the nurse's office. She was in so much pain; she could not stand, could not sit, and could never go back to class. She wasn't sure what hurt worse her tail, or her pride, she cried so hard for both. She missed school for weeks, ole Doc Jones, said she had chipped her tailbone, and to this day, she still could not sit on hard surfaces for very long. Eventually she did have to go back to school and Charlie Cooper was in that class, he had witnessed it all.

She blushed at the memory, "Yes, I remember, now I know why I recognized the house, our school bus used to pass by here and pick you up."

He was one of the nice boys. She pushed the bad memories down, like she always did, and they spent the next half-hour in the lobby catching up on why she had returned to town. He seemed to know all about her, one of Leitchfield's most famous natives. The conversation flowed easily, so when he asked her to join him for dinner at the local steakhouse she excitedly accepted. She did not call this a date, it was catching up with an old acquaintance, it was late in the night when they returned to the B&B. Before the night ended, Charlie invited her to the outdoor concert in the park that Friday night, and she even surprised herself when she said yes.

# SIX

Every night while in Kentucky, she called Leah and filled her in on all the activities, and mentioned Charlie more than once. Leah noticed a new lilt in JW's voice, and couldn't help but tease her a bit. She had never seen JW serious about any man, and it was good to see her happy for once.

JW learned that while she had been busy at Tisch, Charlie had graduated from Texas A&M and joined the Marines. After leaving the Corps, he returned home to run the 300-acre family farm, and help Katie transform the homestead into the Cooper Farm B&B. He had parlayed some smart real estate investments and enjoyed a hefty return. Charlie appeared to be smart, honest, hardworking, and very handsome; JW was surprised to find all those traits in one person, especially in her hometown.

Saturday morning after breakfast, Charlie said, "I have a surprise for you, come with me." He led her outside and there saddled and ready to ride were two beautiful horses.

Charlie said, "You take the white one, she's a little easier to handle."

"Charlie, I haven't sat on a horse since I was 15, and I'll take the roan. If I recall, it's just like ridin a bike," she put her foot in the stirrup, and hopped into the saddle as the horse started running.

When they reached the woods, the horses settled

into a slow walk. The day was early and the dew was still on the ground, causing a mist to rise and swirl from the hills and valleys around them. The horses plodded along the dirt path through the deep woods, as if they had done this a million times before.

After a few hours of enjoying the ride, Charlie said, "Let's take a break, there's a little creek over that a way."

He had brought some supplies in the side packs. Clearly, he had help in this from Katie, as he pulled out baked brie, crackers, grapes, and bottles of water, cloth napkins, and a blanket. After laying the spread out before them, he led the horses to the creek to drink then tied them off to graze while they did likewise on the treats. It was easy being with Charlie, she had never met a man like him before. He was comfortable in his own skin. He never took his eyes off her, but she didn't feel that he was staring at her; it was as if he gazed into her soul.

A light soft summer rain began to fall. They quickly gathered and stowed their picnic. Charlie said, "Hold on tight, it's gonna' get slippery, and try to keep up with me." He slung his leg over his saddle, without even using a stirrup. JW had already mounted and he was two lengths ahead. In the distance, she saw an old rundown house, as the rain pelted harder and lighting started flashing.

They knocked cobwebs down while rushing in through the door with the saddlebags. There clothes were plastered to their bodies, and their hair was dripping wet. Charlie couldn't help but notice JW's white cotton blouse was transparent from the rain.

As she turned to face him, he tried not to stare at her erect brown nipples that showed through her top. He stammered slightly as he said, "It should pass over soon, and we can get back then." JW shivered, and crossed her arms to hide the effects of the cold summer rain. Charlie looked for kindling and paper busying himself by starting a fire in the old fireplace to take the chill off and to calm himself. A soft glow lit up the old house as they sat in front of the fireplace drying themselves, and neither of them was in a hurry to leave this place.

Charlie sat across from her staring into her eyes with the fire to his back. He gently used his fingers to wipe the wet strands of hair off her face and push them behind her ears. She was usually self-conscious of her much too big ears, but right now with him, she didn't care. It was as if he was looking past her physical appearance and deep into her soul. He spoke soft and low, almost in a whisper so as not to break the spell or arouse the spirits swirling around them in the room. The rain pounded on the tin roof, and streams of water dripped onto the floor in areas where the roof had rusted away. Heightened senses gave them goose bumps on their wet skin, and the surroundings didn't matter to them, all they could see was each other's eyes.

The chemistry in the room was palpable. JW pulled out her sketchbook from the saddlebag, and began to sketch Charlie in the glow of the fire. She wanted to capture this moment for a memory for too soon, it would be over and they would be back to reality in the B&B.

That evening she and Charlie went to the concert in the park, the moon was full, and the beer was cold. She had not listened to country music since she had left this town, and it wasn't in her current play list, but when they started the oldies—Unchained Melody by the Righteous Brothers, she was a goner. Charlie grabbed her hand and took her in his arms, put his face in her neck and twirled her around the parking lot turned dance floor. She did not pull away this time, but knew she should. This cannot happen, she thought but they danced on, in each other's arms.

They arrived back at the B&B well after midnight, and tried to sneak in quietly without disturbing the other guest, or Katie. The next morning she realized they failed, when Katie said, "I heard you two come in late last night," with a huge smile on her face. She said, "Charlie doesn't date much, and I'm glad you're here.

Charlie strolled like a cowboy into the room and said, "Today I want to show you something really special. Did you pack a swimsuit? If not, I am sure Katie has one that will fit; you all look to be 'bout the same size. With that, Katie rushed to her room and brought back a one-piece and cover-up, stashed it into a beach bag and hung the bag on Charlie's arm.

"Here you go now git." Katie said, and she pushed them out the door.

When JW asked where they were going, Charlie said, "It's a surprise. But, I hope you like it, it's one of my most favorite places in the whole world," and he turned his truck onto the interstate heading South.

Two hours later, she was on Highway 111 South

in Tennessee, the roadway entering a curve between giant rock walls on each side. They had been talking nonstop the entire drive. She learned that Charlie had joined the Marines when a recruiter showed up at school, and offered him a chance to see the world. Ignorantly, he accepted their offer. During his time in the Corps, he had become a Special Forces Scout Sniper and gone to Ranger School. He had completed tours in Afghanistan before seeing enough war to last a lifetime.

Finally, the truck emerged from between the rock wall, and he said, "Now quickly look to your right." She did, at the same moment they approached a bridge. The view was spectacular. It was the most beautiful water she had ever seen, there was a marina down below and boats bobbed in the lake that snaked as far as the eye could see. She then looked to the left, past Charlie, there were more floating slips, and the lake stretched around a bend in the lake. Thick trees lined the shoreline.

"Welcome to my most favorite place on earth, Dale Hollow Lake, one of the cleanest lakes in the United States, and the best therapy in the world," he said.

She saw green trees and steep hills surrounding the water, no docks, or houses on the pristine waterfront. Charlie told her the entire shoreline is under the jurisdiction of the U.S. Army Corps of Engineers, and there are no houses or disturbances allowed on this lake. It is peaceful, beautiful, and dotted with private coves for 620 miles at summer pool.

41

Charlie said, "I'm proud to say the world record smallmouth bass was pulled out of here in 1955 at over 11 pounds, and that record still holds today." After parking in the lot, he led her down a wooden stairway, across a rickety bridge and down the splintered dock toward a slip where all the large houseboats moored. There was millions of dollars' worth of boats moored in this marina.

Like a proud poppa, he pointed and said, "There's my baby."

JW saw a large houseboat in a slip, a plate on its side noted it was 2019, 100' Custom Sharpe Wide body. Emblazoned on its side in red script was the name 'Liquid Asset'.

Charlie jumped over the rail before her and opened the aluminum gate. He said, "Welcome aboard, my lady," as he extended his hand and helped her onto the sparkling boat.

JW knew it was a huge mistake to cross that gangplank, she felt the urge to run away, but she had nowhere to go but aboard.

# SEVEN

She knew if she took one-step onboard the houseboat, it would be a big mistake. She knew what Charlie expected or wanted, and she could never give either. They could never share a relationship or a life together like Leah and Joseph; their lives were from two different worlds that would never merge—yet, they might collide for an instant, and when they did, it would end in utter destruction for her. For some reason she could not stop walking forward, nor did she want to. Feelings stirred deep within that she had never felt before, and she took his hand.

She said, "thank you Captain, I believe I will."

Charlie raised her outstretched hand to his lips and kissed it. He felt her shudder as he did so and his heart started to pound with excitement. He thought I might have a chance with her, he shook off the feeling and said, "Let me give you the grand tour," as he led her through the large glass doors. She stepped into the salon and saw opulence everywhere; the plush white carpet housed comfortable cream leather theater chairs, facing a large screen TV. The light drew her eyes upward to a wooden box-beamed coffered ceiling, inlaid with mirror tile and featuring a starburst chandelier. As her eyes scanned the interior, tucked into the bow was the starboard controls and computer stations. The open design contained a fully equipped kitchen with stainless appliances, granite countertops with six barstools around a large island. A full bar and stocked wine cooler was contained in the under cabinet design.

"Wow," she said, "I've never seen plush carpet on a boat before, but I'm not sure this is classified as a boat."

"Sure it is," he said.

They continued the tour down the hallway, finding two guest bedrooms and bathroom; at the aft was the main bedroom and private en-suite. Centered on the wall was a massive king-sized bed, piled high with pillows.

She glanced up and saw a large canvas over the bed that looked familiar. It cannot be, she thought to herself, this has to be a copy. She leaned in to see artist's signature, and there—unmistakable, her name, "JW DuValle" in black script. It was hers, an original and one of her favorites, 'The Dancer in Red'. One of the first large works she had sold at Sotheby's, when her work had started attracting serious collectors. The piece had brought mid-six figures, today it would bring over a million, not a bad investment. She was dumbfounded, how long had he been following her, what else did he know about her. She didn't know if she should be happy, or scared, she wasn't quite sure how to react, so she played it cool. Charlie smiled broadly, and said, "I told you I was a big fan."

They continued the tour, outside and off the rear of the boat were two shiny Jet Ski's on a drive on ramp, by the seating area. A spiral ladder led up to the entertainment deck, which housed the grill area, another bar and seating area surrounding a lit and bubbling hot tub. Three large flagpoles flew colors off the rear deck, the U.S. Marine Flag, Old Glory— US Flag and Texas A&M Aggies Flag. No explanation needed.

"Charlie, this is incredible."

"I was hopin' you'd like it, 'cause I sure do," he said. "You can stay in the main bedroom; I'll bunk down the hall. What d'ya say, let's take her out to a cove and I'll show you my lake, and we can relax?"

"I'd be delighted," JW said enthusiastically.

Charlie untied the boat, started the engines, and expertly backed out of the slip into the lane toward the open water, from the fly bridge controls. He made it look effortless, JW was apprehensive; this was a lot of boat to move and no brakes. Charlie floated the behemoth through the no wake zone, past the buoys that separated the million-dollar floating homes from the open channel and out into the open waterway. JW reveled at the sun in her face and wind in her hair.

After 30 minutes of navigating the maze of channels and coves, and JW admiring the beautiful homes built on the cliffs and hillsides. Each of them with magnificent million dollar views overlooking the lake, Charlie coaxed the boat into an isolated cove. He let it drift back into the wooded enclave protected by the forest and rammed the boat aground. The boat screeched to a stop, he hopped down to the front of the boat, and expertly tied off to trees on the bank.

"Here we are." he said raising his arms wide like

he was presenting a gift to her, and she felt like he did.

They foraged in the well-stocked kitchen for snacks and beers from the fridge, changed into their swimsuits and soaked in the hot tub. Conversation was easy between the two of them. They talked about their college years and shared their life stories to this point. A friendship was blooming in the nourishing sun and water of that lake.

Later in the evening, Charlie threw steaks on the grill and cooked them to perfection on the state-of-the-art equipment on the boat. You could tell he was right at home here, and knew what he was doing. JW wondered how many women he had entertained and conquered, as this seemed well rehearsed.

"So, Charlie, do we just stay here all night, how does this work, what's the plan?" She said.

"Oh, I'm sorry. I should have made sure you were ok with staying on the boat until tomorrow. We have Wi-Fi, Cable, and generators, anything you need to connect." He kept talking nervously, "I thought we'd stay tonight and head back to town tomorrow morning so you could make your meeting. Is that OK, if not we can head back? But, we'll need to move fast, because the sun is setting and I don't like to move her at night. Not a lot of people can navigate in the dark and you never know who might plow into you." He explained.

"I guess, it'll be ok, I have a cell signal. I just wanted to call my friend Leah later tonight." She said.

"For now, how about we take a dip in the lake and let you float your cares away a bit?" He said.

"Now you're talking." JW went to put on her borrowed suit.

When she came out of the bathroom, she realized by Charlie's smile, the suit fit her perfectly and Katie had great taste. She made a running dive off the back of the boat into the warm, clear water. A taut and tan Charlie dove in after her and they splashed each other and floated, in the warm water soaking up the sun.

Later that evening on the top-deck, they watched as the sun set behind the treetops. The colors in the sky spoke to her with their artistry, and it looked like the creator painted it especially for her. The reds were vibrant and oranges looked like flames shooting out from the sun that sat as a ball of fire in the center. The trees were casting shadows, which enveloped around them, and cooled the night air. The crickets and bullfrogs turned out in full force. Their evening performance brought a cacophony of sounds trying to drown out the buzzing of insects drawn to the nightlights of the boat.

Soon, it was pitch dark and a full moon appeared, Charlie said, "I want to show you something spectacular." He pulled their lounge chairs to an open area on the top, where there was nothing separating them from the night sky and the stars. "Now lay back and look up." She had never seen such bright stars, since they were not vying with city lights. He said, "I practice Sabaism—the worship of stars." He laughed as he began pointing out the constellations to her. "There's the big dipper, 'Ursa Major', and there's the little dipper, 'Ursa Minor', see it? There's 'Cassiopeia', that's a little harder to make out." He gently opened her hand and traced the stars on her palm. He then raised her palm to his mouth and kissed it so tenderly, letting his lips caress her skin softly, stirring her imagination. Both of them were breathing rapidly, even though the night air was chilly. Their bodies were reacting to what their minds were anticipating, and their temperatures rose. The air around them was hot, and their breathing heavy.

JW was torn, she wanted with all she had to lean into him and feel his lips and rough chin on her face and body and make passionate love to him all night under the moon and stars, giving in to him freely and completely. She was weakening to his charms and pursuit. She had never experienced such intimacy with a man, and she wanted more with Charlie. Her body ached with the stirred desire and a longing to love someone without holding back. All her life she had protected her heart, she vowed she would never open herself to love and loss again. Yet, now she was so close to giving herself to Charlie completely, she longed for a love like that. At the very moment, she was ready to let her inhibitions go; then she realized the repercussions and became afraid.

Jerking away she said, "No, Charlie we can't."

Composing herself, she said, "I have a really big day tomorrow, and I need to call Leah. So, I'm going below and I'll see you for breakfast around 8?" With that she was gone, she ran away again to her safe space below.

Charlie blew out a breath, and doubled over to hide his throbbing arousal and wondered what damage had he done to their relationship.

# EIGHT

Early Monday afternoon JW sat in the law office of Shore and Shore, but her mind was still on a houseboat in the middle of the lake. She could not get Charlie out of her mind, and body, she tingled each time her mind drifted back to their night under the stars.

Promptly at 1 PM the lawyer, she assumed the one that called her, entered the room. He said, "I am expecting another party to arrive, apparently they are running behind, so let's give it 10 more minutes, if that's ok with you?" Immediately, she froze, she knew the only other person it could be—Cousin Luther.

"Mr. Woosley, I assume, we are waiting for my cousin Luther Decker?"

"Why, yes, we are." He said.

"You are aware that he is a convicted felon?" She quickly added, "I am very uncomfortable being in the same room with him, we have, um—shall I say history."

"No worries, he's on parole and has been out for over two years, on his best behavior. He knows if he slips up, he goes back to Eddyville for the balance of a life sentence." He said.

She jumped up, ready to bolt, just as the outside door opened and in walked a living, breathing, and nightmare: Cousin Luther. He blocked her exit and she backed into the farthest corner, shaking while trying to maintain composure.

"Well, if'n it ain't my fancy sweet cuz, Wanda Jane. As if'n I live 'n breathe? My how you've changed, I haven't seen you for, what over'n 20 yars now." Luther said in his hick vernacular.

JW could not bring herself to speak; she just nodded slightly and blocked her body with her purse, so he could not leer at her. After he sat at the table, on the side near her, she moved to another chair nearest the exit. She refused to appear like a scared rabbit in a room with this predator, she thought.

The attorney was unaware of the palpable tension. He began the meeting and started to read, "This is the last will and testament of Mrs. Minnie Decker Davis. I being of sound mind…"

At that point, Luther said very obnoxiously, "cut to the chase man, I don't wanna hear all that mumbo jumbo…what did she leave me? And what is she a do'in har." He angrily jabbed his index finger with a dirty fingernail toward JW, as if it were a gun.

"Mr. Decker, your mother, has named both of you in her last will and testament. We can forgo the reading and I can summarize for you." He paused, "You have been given the balance of her checking and savings account, which amounts to $5,443.15, and all furniture and assets in the homestead farm, which she owned outright, and you will need to remove those forthwith." He said. Luther smiled showing the gaping holes where teeth used to reside.

"Ms. DuValle, bequeathed to you is the family farm homestead, consisting of all land and improvements, comprising 150 acres. I believe you know the address?"

Luther yelled as he jumped to his feet, "what in tha hell, dya' mean? That's ma' land, s'posed to be mine! She cheated me outta what's mine."

JW stood, jutted out her chin, placed her hands flat down on the tabletop, leaning toward him with a stern expression and said, "Not anymore, it's not." She quickly turned and walked out the door, saying to the lawyer as she walked, "Draw up the papers I need to sign, I'll settle up with you before I leave town. Thanks." She flipped a wave over her shoulder as she left.

She heard Luther mutter under his breath, "You bitch, I'll get you for this. I know all about you now. I know whar ya' live and how t' find ya'. You won't get away with this."

Shaking so badly she could hardly get the key in the ignition, she started the car and quickly backed out of the parking lot and headed back to the B&B as fast as she could drive. When she pulled into B&B, she realized her hands gripped the steering wheel until her knuckles turned white, while tears streamed down her face. She practiced the calming breathing techniques she had learned in years of counseling, wiped her tears away, and walked bravely to her room.

She called Leah immediately. "Leah, you won't believe what happened." She excitedly recounted the story, barely stopping to catch her breath between sentences.

"JW, I am so proud of you, schatzeleh. However,

you need to be careful and get back here as soon as you can. Oh wait, I have an even better idea, I need to come to you. I have to meet this person, Charlie. He sounds like the real deal. I am booking a ticket now; you can pick me up at the airport in Louisville. I've always wanted to visit the South." Leah said.

When Leah called JW her pet name schatzeleh— 'little treasure' in Yiddish, she knew that she was proud of her. She also knew that Luther was dangerous and meant what he said too. She needed to watch her back from here on out. Having Leah here would help her to do that too, and she smiled when she thought of Leah meeting Charlie. That is gonna be a real hoot, New York Jew meets Kentucky.

Then she realized she had not even thought about the farm. The farm had belonged to her grandparents. Aunt Minnie paid the past due taxes on the land when they had died and gotten title to the whole shebang. Momma and Daddy did not have money to pay their share, so she took it all. The farm had taken more from her than it ever gave her, and the tiny house upon that land was featured front and center in her nightmares. She shuddered and tried to block out the flashbacks of that terrible, no-good, bad summer when she was nine. She thought what sweet justice that it now belonged to her. She had an axe to grind with that barn and that house, and as soon as it was legally hers to do with as she pleased, she planned to deliver on the promise she made to herself long ago.

When Charlie came in from the field that evening,

he lightly pecked at her door. She cracked it open, and saw him leaning against the doorjamb. God, she thought as her belly flopped, this man is so sweet and sexy, and he smells good too.

"Well hello there beautiful," he said in that soft southern drawl.

"Hello there, to you too", she whispered back, leaning on the opposing doorjamb.

"What you say, we get out of here for a while, maybe grab a bite to eat?" Charlie said.

"I have an idea," she says, "why don't we take a drive out by the farm I inherited today?" His eyebrows shot up, "Wow that sounds like a plan shall we?" He then extended his arm and led her away.

Charlie knew exactly where the farm was located, and he drove down the gravel lane and pulled into the drive that peaked on the top of a very steep hill. She had to fight gravity to keep the door open, as she hopped out of the jacked-up pickup truck. She stood flatfooted and stared at the dilapidated front porch, the old house badly needed a coat of paint, and the windows shot out from local kids with BB guns, and the ragged curtains blowing in the summer breeze.

What she came to see, was not in that house or barn, she walked toward the backfield with Charlie beside her. She found the family graveyard; there was the flat stone of her first Uncle. She brushed off the dirt and mud and took a photo of the name carved on the home made stone. Next to his grave, was Aunt Minnie's resting place, the earth had not yet been packed down by the rains, and was mostly large clots of red clay. A few feet away, she saw her father and mother's grave with a small granite stone declaring their births, deaths and wedding dates. It was then she noticed, her mother's maiden name was the same as Aunt Minnie's first married name. What, she thought, as she snapped a photo of the evidence, this would explain a lot. She traced the names etched in her parents' stone with her trembling fingers.

Charlie said, "You know they would be so proud of you, don't you?"

"I guess." She said as she stood up. "We better go, I'm hungry, how about you?"

"Wanda Jane, you are one strange and beautiful bird." Charlie smiled as he took her hand in his to walk back toward the truck.

# NINE

After the meeting in the shyster attorney's office Luther craved a stiff drink. He headed his old beat-up truck for the Sugar Shack, a hole in the wall on the outskirts of town that had one of the few drive-thru liquor stores in Leitchfield. As a parolee, he was not to enter a bar, possess, or use alcoholic beverages. Hell he thought, I don't care, I deserve a drink after today. He bought a six-pack of Budweiser to take back to the house, and a fifth of the cheapest whiskey he could get for immediate use.

If caught for a parole violation, he would find himself back at the 'Castle on the Cumberland' for the remainder of his 30 year to life sentence. He already served 15 of the 30-year sentence, and he had no desire to let the state provide free room and board for the balance of that term. He had to keep his nose clean, pass his drug tests, and keep a job. He had succeeded at none of those things yet.

"That prissy bitch," he said aloud as he thought of Wanda and today's events. The more he drank the more he cursed Wanda Jane's existence.

"She thinks she's too good to be from around here, she's always had it easy. I'm gonna make her pay," he said to no one, as he drank more as he drove down the winding country road back to his lodging.

A tragic childhood had brought Luther to this lot in life; he was the product of an incestuous coupling of cousins, Minnie and Roger Decker. That fact alone had robbed him of several IQ points. Add to that Luther's daddy had not been a kind man, he was a drunkard and abuser of women, animals, and children, which included Luther. He did not spare his offspring or his wife from 'the rod' and his violent outburst and mistreatment. Luther still bore the scar he received when he was but four years old, after a run-in one evening with drunken, dear old dad. The weapon was an iron poker used to stoke the fire in the potbelly stove, which heated the three-room shack they called home. One minute Luther was crying for something like small kids do, the next minute he heard a crack, was seeing blackness and stars with blood dripping down his face, and had the worst headache. The wound began over his left eye and ran down to his cheekbone. After the first blow and his blood-curdling squall, Aunt Minnie stepped between father and son, grappled with Roger for the poker, and the rest is a blur as Luther blacked out. Luther never got stitches that he could remember, and the scar was evidence of that fact. He was never 'right in the head', as Momma said, after the attack. He did remember flashbacks of people crying, his Momma dragging daddy to the yard by the legs, and a dark hole in the ground. The mean man was no more, but neither was young Luther.

Cousin Luther never seemed to catch a break either. As the story goes, when he was ten there was a coonhound tied out in back of the house, and Luther was told by his latest new 'uncle daddy' not to go near the dog. It had been acting strange, barking, and foaming around the mouth when anyone got near and it was vicious. However, dim-witted Luther did not follow directions very well. He was being mean and teasing the dog, and got within reach of the chained animal. The dog attacked, grabbing him by the face, mauling him and dragging him toward its doghouse. Aunt Minnie heard before she saw the carnage, she grabbed a .22 rifle they kept in the corner, and ran toward the doghouse. She grabbed the boy's leg and pulled, there was a tug-o-war between her and the dog for the limp body. She squatted down over her boy, put the gun to the dogs head, and shot it dead. They did take Luther to the hospital this time, autopsied the dog's brains, and found it to be harboring rabies. They cleaned and patched the bites, and he suffered through 21 painful injections of rabies vaccine given into his stomach over several days. This ordeal probably accounted for a loss of a few more IQ points, and cousin Luther already had none to spare.

The time came when Luther had gone too far and was finally convicted of a major crime. No amount of bribery to the local, good ole boys like in the past would get him out of this one. Since a teen, he was always in trouble with the local law, however, this time the State Boys were involved. Right before JW left for New York, she had overhead Momma and Aunt Minnie talking about Luther's latest run in with the law. Of course, Aunt Minnie said he was innocent, as usual, but like all the times before, he clearly was not.

Back in those days, Grayson County was a 'dry'

county. It had been that way since the prohibition. Luther was raised in this Kentucky culture of coon hunting, moonshining, bootlegging, and evading the law. Even killing rivals if necessary. Many of the locals made what little money they had running stills and selling the illegal liquor made in the light of the moon, hence its name as 'moonshine'. The stills were set up deep in the woods near running water and out of sight, the process was a round the clock event. Many of the 'shiners' had an old custom of coon hunting. These hill people would run their bloodhounds all night, tree a coon, and harvest the meat and pelt. There was also one other cherished item they harvested from the male raccoon. The penis bone, it was used to plug the copper tubing allowing the collection to flow smoothly into the collection bucket.

When the locals could not brew enough of the needed 'hooch' to meet demand, some of the boys would rev up their old cars and make a run to nearby towns, most frequently Bowling Green. They built the cars fast to outrun the police, and many of the original NASCAR circuit racers got their start running bootleg liquor from the law in the area.

The event that won Luther's all-expense paid trip to Eddyville was due to an unfortunate run in with a fellow bootlegger. The man had owed Luther money for a liquor run, he had collected from the buyer's and instead of paying Luther his part, the man decided to invest in the up and coming new drug of choice in the area—cooking meth. Rumor has it that Luther, while trying to collect his money, picked up a brick lying beside the front porch steps, and proceeded to beat the man to death. The State Police caught him in the act. In order to save the state time and money, he pled down from second-degree murder to first-degree manslaughter. He received parole after serving 15 years of hard time.

He came out of prison with no front teeth, prison tats, a case of HIV, and a lot of anger as a hardened criminal. Now he was back in town, vowing to make Wanda Jane pay, and Luther was a man that had nothing to lose.

# TEN

After the run-in with Luther at the attorney's office, she was a nervous wreck. She vomited in the toilet, washed her face, brushed her teeth, and tried to pull herself together. She turned to her sketchpad to ease her mind; she felt it calling to her. Lately, her sketches were mostly of Charlie, she found him a perfect example of the male form. He was as pleasing on the paper as well as in her mind. He was gorgeous, and polite, and sweet, and romantic, and rich.....
"Just stop," she muttered under her breath.

She couldn't focus on the paper, her mind raced from one topic to the next. I need to talk to Leah, she thought. Leah was her calming port in the midst of the storm, answering on the first ring, "Ahava, I have missed you so much, what is happening there?"

JW smiled when she heard her pet name, it meant 'Love' in Hebrew, and she knew Leah meant it. Quickly she remembered why she called, "I'm in over my head Leah. My crazy cousin just threatened to kill me, and he will. He knows my new name, where I live, everything I have tried to hide for all these years. I think I made a big mistake coming back here."

Leah said, "JW, you are not the little girl you were when you left there, you are a strong, beautiful and successful woman. You need to remember that. Just be smart, don't be alone."

"But, Leah, you don't understand, even if he doesn't hurt me he could ruin my life and my career—everything I have worked for all these years," she cried. "He knows things, bad things I've never told anyone. Maybe I should just come home and forget all this."

"JW, stop, just stop it, now. I will come down to you, and we will face this together. There is nothing you could ever do to make me quit loving you, believe that, and believe in yourself," Leah said. "I'll send you my travel arrangements via text in a few minutes; pick me up at the airport, and get me a room." JW had learned, when Leah makes up her mind there is no arguing against her, when she barks orders, you just do it.

After they chatted for a few more minutes and then hung up, she realized she had not seen Charlie today, so she paid a visit to Katie at the front desk.

"Hi Katie, where's that handsome brother of yours?"

"Um, he had some business to take care of at the trucking company today, he'll be late," she said.

"Trucking company? That's the first I've heard of that," she said, "he owns a trucking company?" She asked incredulously, thinking he is a man of many talents.

"Yeah, you know Charlie," she said. "He always has a new business idea cooking. He started Cooper Trucking in 2015, a year after daddy passed. He started very small with a couple of trucks and now he has about 125 trucks, 200 trailers, and 50 people in the office at last count, he probably won't be in tonight until really late. I think he said he had a load coming up from the Mexico corridor."

"Oh, well," her voice trailed. "Katie, I'm a little spooked after the run-in I had at the lawyer today. My cousin was there and he is really pissed that the division of property did not go as he planned. So can you keep an eye out for anybody poking around here that doesn't belong?"

"Sure, we have security alarms on all the doors and windows, and all kinds of cameras around the property. Charlie has topnotch security, with his background in Marine Special Ops. Don't worry he's always on the watch for the bad guys," she said.

"Also, changing the subject, I need a room for my friend coming in later this week. Her name is Leah Levy." Katie's demeanor changed—or did it? Had JW just misread her body language? Did she just make a grimace? JW said, "Don't worry about special diet. She is modern Orthodox, just don't serve any pork and don't mix the dairy with any meat and it'll be ok. I want her to be comfortable here; she is like a sister to me. Thanks for everything," JW said as she walked back to her room.

Katie's stony gaze followed her back to her door, no words, no smile.

It had been a trying day for JW. Surely, she had not perceived any anti-Semitism in her conversation with Katie, had she? She was seeing shadows everywhere, and she was spooked and paranoid.

The next day she had to sign papers and pick up the deed to the farm, so she decided to turn in early and try to forget all about today. She also prayed she would never have to see Luther again.

The next morning after breakfast, JW walked to her car in the drive and was dumbfounded to see she had a flat tire. What, not possible, she had four flat tires.

"What in the hell?" she said aloud. Upon closer inspection there appeared to be a puncture on the outside of each tire, the rear driver side still had a hunting knife imbedded in the tire, holding a note written with poor grammar. It said in large black letters, GO HOME. YOUR KIND DON'T BELONG HERE!

JW grabbed the knife wrenching it out of the tire, along with the note and stomped back to the front desk. "Katie, what in the hell is this? Pull up the video and see who did this," she ordered.

"Who did what?" Katie asked wide-eyed.

"Some piece of shit slit all four of my tires. Why would somebody do this?" She said.

"Oh damn," as she pulled up the video on the computer screen. "Well, that's strange," she said. "The recording is blank, there's nothing there. It looks like it malfunctioned last night. I am so sorry. Do you want to call the cops? I'm gonna call Charlie."

"No, just call a tow truck." JW knew who did it, Luther, but she had no proof, what good would the cops do.

After replacing the tires, JW drove nervously to the attorney's office. She was constantly checking her rearview mirror to see if anyone was following her. They had all the papers ready for filing and after she had paid for the legal work, the clerk handed her a sheaf of papers. "What's all this?" She asked.

"That's your new deed we're filing at the courthouse, and your survey, along with a plat drawing," the clerk advised. She opened the survey for JW, lay it on the table, and pointed to the property JW had inherited.

It showed the parcel boundaries, the shape, and size of the parcel, and the name of the owner of record for the land surrounding her new farm.

"Well, this is news. I did not realize the Cooper Family Farm adjoined my property at the backside. Is that the Charlie Cooper Farm?" She asked.

"Yes, that's what this says, so yes," the clerk answered. She added, "What makes this interesting is that your property has all this road frontage, all the Cooper Farm has is an easement through your property. That's represented by this symbol on the plat map, you should also have it written somewhere in your deed, spelling out the legal ramifications granting the easement. Of course, they can enter by the backside, but that's not direct access to the county highway, or interstate."

"Hmmm, that's strange; Charlie never mentioned this to me. Well, all right then, I guess it just slipped his mind. He is a busy fella. Thanks, for your help." JW left the office with more questions than when she arrived, and had an ominous feeling in her gut.

# ELEVEN

JW realized she was hungry, so she grabbed carryout and headed back to the B&B, not sure, if she would see Charlie tonight or if he would blow her off again. Due to her day, she was in a foul mood.

She noticed Charlie's truck was in the drive when she pulled up, and her demeanor lifted at the thought of seeing him. She then reprimanded herself for thinking about anything more than a friendship with this guy. She was not in the market for a relationship, with anyone, especially anyone from this town.

Charlie was waiting in the lobby for her, and stood when she walked in the door.

"Oh man, I knew I should have called and asked you to dinner earlier," he said deflated.

"I've got takeout, but there's enough to share, if you want? General Tso's chicken and fried rice." She said.

Charlie got paper plates and silverware from the kitchen, and they sat in the dining room.

"You like Chinese?" She said. He nodded.

As they dug into the food and stuffed it into their mouths, Charlie said, "Tell me about your day, I missed you yesterday. I'm sorry I didn't call I had a long day."

"Not much happened, other than a slasher took out my tires and left me a love letter. It was probably that psycho cousin of mine." She said.

"I heard." He muttered between bites with cheeks full like a chipmunk, cute she thought.

She assumed Katie must have filled him in on all the details and she just wanted to forget about it, so she quickly changed the subject.

"Oh, and I got the deed to the farm yesterday, it's all settled. But, an interesting tidbit, did you know that our land meets on the backside? I got a survey with the papers, and the plat shows the landowners for adjoining property." Charlie looked surprised at her revelation and turned a bit red, but maybe her eyes were playing tricks on her in the dim lighting. She admonished herself, JW, you have to quit being so paranoid.

"I seem to recall that now that you mention it, I had forgotten all about that." He said.

Alarm bells sounded in her head, and she wasn't sure why. However, one thing she had learned, and that was to trust her gut. Something is not quite right about this, but she couldn't put her finger on it—yet.

Segueing the conversation again, "Katie tells me you have a trucking company, Charlie, I am so surprised, you never said a word. Tell me all about it." She said.

"Not much to tell," he said on an exhale. "I started the business after I came back from the Marines, right before Daddy died. He kinda' helped put the plan in motion and the business just took off. You know the Marine Raider moto, 'Always Faithful, Always Forward.' We started up in 2015. It just kept growing and picking up more lines and the fleet got bigger and bigger. It has grown fast, I've been real lucky." He said.

"Something tells me it's not all luck." She said.

"Well, what's that supposed to mean?" He said defensively.

"I-I-I didn't mean anything bad, just that you are a hard-working and intelligent man. It cannot all be luck, that's all. You earned your success." She stammered, and felt oddly reprimanded.

Charlie sensed from her reaction, that he had gone too far. He was being oversensitive to her offhand remark. She didn't know anything. "I'm sorry, JW, I'm just really tired and edgy tonight. Let's call it a day and I'll see you in the morning for breakfast, about 8?"

"Sure thing," she said as she cleared the table and put the trash in the garbage.

This conversation prompts another late night phone call to Leah, she thought; she will need her help and connections for what she was planning. One thing JW had learned from her years in New York City, trust no one. She returned to her room and called her best friend.

"Leah, I need to hire somebody to do a background check on my old friend, Charlie. Something is not quite right here, but I can't figure out what. It may be nothing, but my gut is telling me something stinks," she said.

"I know a guy, Joseph used him once, and he is pretty deep undercover. This person can find out anything. What do you want to know, Zeeskeit?"

"I just love it when you call me honey and do whatever I ask." JW laughed.

She continued, "You have Charlie's name and address, he's my age, graduated in 2002, and says he was in Marines from 2007 – 2015. He's clearly not telling me everything though."

"OK, I'll ask Joseph to start right now. You be careful, Keh Neged—'against the evil eye', I am spitting…Ptu, ptu, ptu….I'm getting scared for you."

JW laughed, at Leah's fake spitting 3 times at the evil eye, "I'm fine, just get here soon, goodnight and sweet dreams sister."

The next morning Charlie was in a better mood, and he was trying to makeup to JW for his shitty attitude last night. He admitted he was rude, apologized and asked her to dinner that evening. She accepted and after he left, she poured another cup of coffee and sat on the front porch looking out at the green fields taking in the country smells, deep in thought.

"Mind if I join you?" Katie asked as she sat down in the rocker next to her, sipping her hot coffee.

"I'd love company. But, you have to tell me more about your brother, if you do. He really is getting to me. So, what am I walking in to?" She said.

"Well, he is an anomaly that's for sure. Ummm, let's see—he graduated with you in 2002, went off to college, and then joined the Marine Corps, served in Afghanistan. I never thought he would be back here, but he just showed up one summer day and said, I'm home. We were really shocked, but that's Charlie." Katie said.

"He never had a 'significant other', in all these years?" JW asked.

"Well there was a girl back in high school, she was a preppy, cheer leader, and she treated him real bad. Her name is Brenda Johnson; she cheated on Charlie with a football player, and broke his heart. When Charlie loves, he loves deep." She looked right in JW's face when she said that.

She paused briefly, then continued, "When he came back home, she tried to cozy up to him again. He won't have anything to do with her, but she keeps trying. She is not so hot now; she drives a school bus, divorced, 2 kids, and not the looker she was in high school. But, that's not why Charlie won't get with her; it's because of how she did him in school. He does hold a grudge, and he can be very hard." Katie said.

"Oh, I remember Brenda; she was behind us a couple years in school. She was pretty; I wasn't caught up in the drama of high school. I had my sights set on getting out of here, and also just trying to make it day to day." JW Said.

"You know JW, there's something you need to know about Charlie, that does involve your past." She said.

JW froze, she knows about my past, her heart starting pounding in her ears and she was sure she flushed.

"When Charlie was in 8th grade, he got in trouble, he got arrested for battery. He was expelled from school for a week. He almost didn't get accepted into college over it." Katie rocked gently and did not take her gaze off the fields in front of her, as she continued. "It seems there was an incident in one of his classes. Some jerk boy pulled a chair out from under a girl injuring her real bad, and all the boys that thought they were hot stuff laughed. Charlie got pissed—he has a temper you know. Well, he cleaned that boy's clock. The kid was a lot bigger than Charlie was too, but he didn't care. Right there in class in front of God n'everybody he knocked him out with one lick, but he didn't stop hitting the kid. He beat him bad, coupla' black eyes, bloodied his nose, and chipped a tooth. Of course, they expelled him and he got probation. Daddy was so mad at Charlie. That is, until Daddy found out why he did it, and then he wasn't so mad anymore. Charlie was always trying to make Daddy proud, he still is, but that is hard to do. Damn near impossible, if you ask me." Katie said.

JWs mouth was open, "I-I-I didn't know. Katie, that girl was me."

Katie just shook her head, and said, "Yeah," she knew all along.

Immediately JW felt bad for doubting Charlie. She was going to call Leah later today and cancel the background check. What was she thinking, oh, I am such an idiot sometimes.

"I think I'm going to drive around town, and check out some old friends of my mother's, I haven't seen in a long, long, time, if they are still alive." JW said as she got up and slowly walked to the car. She was very sad as she thought about the ripples of pain and trouble her life has brought to so many people around her.

# TWELVE

At least today, there was no knife in her tire, she chuckled, and the day was beautiful. She planned to pay a visit to her mom's old friend, Mrs. Darby, if she was still alive. She is about her mother's age, so that would make her in her 70's; so she is probably still kickin' she thought.

Mrs. Darby ran the general store called the 'Sunfish Mall'. It really wasn't a mall at all, but a one room run-down collection of stuff the local's might need to buy in a pinch, and a deli. Back when she was a child, before the new Walmart or Dollar General was built; the Sunfish Mall is where people would shop between monthly grocery runs to the big city of Bowling Green or Elizabethtown. The Sunfish Mall was what kept her and Momma alive. God bless Mrs. Darby, and credit.

As she drove toward the country road near the farm, she reminisced of the past and Mrs. Darby helping her select groceries momma needed from the shelves. Her list was usually scribbled on a piece of brown paper sack or the back of an envelope, which previously held a bill. Wanda would reach high over her head and push the shopping cart down each aisle of the country store, trying the best a 6-year-old could do to decipher the scribble on the paper to match a can. Momma had tried to teach her how to know the best value, and to consider serving size and price before putting the cans in the basket. When she couldn't make out the words, Mrs. Darby would phone Momma and ask her what she wanted. She had to be careful how much she bought, because she had to load-up the Radio Flyer wagon and pull the load home too. Every now and then, Mrs. Darby would ask another shopper to give Wanda a ride home, saying, "You go right past her house, how about you take her home?" She would say, as if it was just a natural thing.

After Wanda made her selection, she had to hoist the stuff onto the counter, while Mrs. Darby rang up the goods. Wanda loved to watch her push those buttons and then hit the long bar on the side with her palm. She hoped someday she could get a job like that. But, her most favorite thing was to watch the bagboy, put her groceries in the sacks. He always joked and kidded with her. She had such a crush on that boy; she tried her best to remember his name.....drew a blank. Wanda never had money to pay for the food; Mrs. Darby let them pay 'on account'. She always thought that meant, 'on account' because we was poor. After tallying our bill, she would turn the receipt over, and Wanda would do her best forgery of her Daddy's name. Once a month after Daddy was paid, he'd go in and pay down the bill.

As far as JW knew, they might still owe Mrs. Darby money. She'd have to rectify that if so, and she'd love to speak to someone that knew her Momma. She still missed her after all these years.

JW drove up to the front of the dilapidated

building; the porch looked like an old scarecrow someone had tried to brace up in a field with a couple of posts. The roof was hanging crookedly. The paint was peeling off the front of the building, and there were old rusted signs hung across the front-telling people to 'Drink Coca Cola' and various other advertisements. The front door was screen wire that had seen better days, bowed out in places where hands had pushed for many years. The bottom half was a 'Rainbow Bread' sign. The lights appeared to be on inside the store. Good she thought, someone is still around that might know Mrs. Darby.

When she opened the screen, a tiny bell rang out to announce her presence. She drew a sharp breath at the smells and memories it evoked. To the left was the deli area, behind a large glassed in refrigerator. Like a modern butcher shop, she saw rolls of country food: baloney, 'head cheese' or souse, liverwurst, yellow American cheese, sitting there waiting to be sliced. Just looking at the assortment brought back familiar smells and memories of Momma making Daddy sandwiches to take in his lunch. Trying her best to get me to "just try a bite, you might like it." She shook her head, to dislodge the memory, nasty still she thought.

Walking straight towards the back of the store, there was still a large pot-bellied stove with kindling sticking out of a barrel beside it. To the right were four small tables, with four chairs per table, and over the top on each table was a red-checkered greasy laminated tablecloth. Each table held a checkers board game and a dog-eared used deck of cards, along with salt and peppershakers. There was also, a large barrel to the left of the stove, it said 'Pickle Barrel' on the side, and had a wooden lid with a handle. She guessed it was self-serve pickles. That was new. Located to the right of the room was a unisex, one toilet bathroom. JW poked her head in to check it out—this was new too, there was no bathroom when she last visited. It wasn't much to look at, a dirty sink bolted to the wall, an old-fashioned roller towel dispenser hung—which didn't hold towels anymore, a ratty toilet with brown stained pee rings in the bowl. The floor was filthy, and looked like it had not been cleaned since it was installed; the toilet had small drops of urine that bleached the wood floor. Somebody didn't have good aim, or they had dribbles, she thought. The room carried the accompanying stench.

She continued her self-guided tour; down each aisle, she walked looking at all the dusty cans and yellowed bags and boxes. Some of this product was clearly outdated. It sure was different from what she remembered.

She spotted the drink chest, and she remembered every now and then that Momma would let her splurge and buy a grape or orange NeHi soda. She opened the lid to disappointment. It was empty and not working. Apparently, it was an antique now, and used as a prop just like the 'Pickle Barrel' for the out of towners that wanted the real 'Old Country Store' experience.

She approached the counter by the cash register, and there seated on a stool, she could not believe her eyes—sat Mrs. Darby. She hadn't changed at all. The first thing you noticed about her was her ample bosom, which called attention to her short arms. She still wore the same type of clothes, loud and vibrant florals. Today she wore a Cerulean blue top and matching slacks. Amazingly, her hair was still the same color, store bought boxed coppery red, all teased up and twisted into curls, and lacquered with hairspray so it would not move. She wore powder blue eye shadow, with painted on eyebrows and bright red lipstick, and big round earrings with every color you could imagine in them.

JW said, "Mrs. Darby, I'd know you anywhere, you haven't changed a bit."

Mrs. Darby looked puzzled at JW and smiled, clearly not recognizing this stranger standing before her and calling her by name. She said with a nervous laugh in her voice, "I'm sorry, child, but I can't seem to place you? Who be you?"

"It's me Mrs. Darby, Wanda Jane. Don't you remember me?" She said timidly.

"Honey, child, it can't be. Get around her girl and let me get a good look at you. Oh, my, what a beautiful young woman you turned out to be. What in the world are you doing here?" The words and questions just kept coming out of her mouth; JW didn't even have time to answer one question before another one popped up.

Finally, Mrs. Darby stepped out from behind the counter and said, "let's go sit on the porch for a spell and catch up." She took JW by the elbow and led her to the front porch and they sat there on the old church pew up against the warped boards and talked about her life and reason for coming back visit to Sunfish Mall.

Mrs. Darby said, "I wish your Momma and Daddy could see you now, how you turned out. I've wondered about you, wondered if you were ok, and had a home and someone to love and take care of you. You were such a sweet and innocent that had to deal with a lot of life as a little girl." Tears welled up in her eyes. "I sure loved your sweet momma. We were best friends, even if just over the phone."

"I know, and I need to know if you need anything? How can I repay all the kindness you showed to me and my family?" JW said, "I've had some success in life and I have money, how can I help you?"

"Child you don't owe me a thing, I'm so touched you remember me after all these years, I only wish I could have done more for you and your Momma. It seems like it was never enough." She said.

"Mrs. Darby, I came here to tell you that you made a difference in my life, you helped me when I didn't even know I needed it. Thank you. I will always be grateful to you for your kindness." JW hugged her fiercely.

When they broke apart, Mrs. Darby said, "Child I need to tell you that there is some bad people around here, that don't want an outsider nosing around. It's not healthy. You may have grown up here, but you don't belong here no more. You need to be careful, and watch your back, and get out of town as fast as you came. There's still some old beliefs buried deep in this town. People are not what they seem to be, that's all I can say about that; but, heed my warning child, it's dangerous here and that cousin of yours is bad news. He killed a man with his bare hands you know. I wouldn't put anything past him."

"You don't need to warn me about Luther, I know firsthand how bad he is." She said as she stiffened up and pulled away as if some old memory pulled her back into darkness.

"It's not just Luther; things are not always as they seem at first glance." And with that warning, Mrs. Darby stood and embraced JW like she used to do when she was a little girl and for a minute it felt like Momma was hugging her again. It felt good.

# THIRTEEN

Today was the day Leah would finally arrive, she was flying into the Louisville airport, JW was to pick her up, and she reserved her a room at the B&B. She was so excited, she could hardly wait to see her friend; it had been 10 days since she had arrived in town and desperately needed to see another friendly New York face.

This was going to be a great three-day weekend; she planned to show her the farm and area where she grew up, and to meet Charlie. Of course, if there was to be any future between the two of them, he had to win Leah over too. Tonight they had dinner plans at the B&B with Katie and Charlie. Saturday morning Charlie was to take them to the annual Twin Lakes Fiddle Festival, which was beginning at the town square. In addition to the annual contest, there would be vendor booths, crafts, carnival rides, an antique car cruise-in, followed by a free concert. The streets around the square would close and traffic rerouted around the square. This would be perfect timing for Leah to experience small town Americana in the south, and be a culture shock for a Jewess from New York City. After the festival, Charlie had invited them both to spend the night on the houseboat. JW couldn't wait to see Leah's reaction to the lake.

The flight and drive to Leitchfield went off without a hitch, JW couldn't believe how nervous she was to show her friend her hometown, and especially introduce her to Charlie. He had promised he would be home in time, showered, shaved, and ready for their arrival. When she pulled into the drive, she was not surprised to see his truck.

When Leah exited the car she said, "I can see why you like this place, it's absolutely charming, and so green. Look there is a real live cow. I have never been this close to a cow before; I've only seen them on TV and in books. It's amazing, I have to get a picture of this," she said as she pulled out her cell phone and snapped a photo. She then bent down to smell the deep purple lavender growing along the walk, and snapped another photo.

"I told you, it was beautiful," JW said.

Charlie bounded out the door when the two women approached the steps, "Let me take that suitcase for you and introduce myself. Hi, I'm Charlie." He extended his hand to shake hers.

Leah was immediately impressed, he was as handsome as JW said he was, and he smelled like fresh soap and clean linen, with a hint of a killer aftershave. Yum, she thought.

Katie was in the kitchen, banging dishes, and hurriedly placing final additions on the meal. She shouted over the clanging pots, "Dinner will be ready in about 15 minutes, go get washed up and come to the dining room."

The atmosphere at dinner was exciting and the conversation flowed freely, as did the wine. JW was happy, the laughter was loud, and she felt at home and surrounded by love. This seemed right to her.

They all pitched in and helped Katie clean up the kitchen, then retreated to the front porch to watch the fireflies light up the night. Charlie lit up a stogie. If that is his only bad habit, I guess I can overlook that, thought JW. The conversation never waned, but most of the talk was about JW's college years, and early success. Leah was impressed when she learned Charlie was in possession of "The Dancer in Red" painting, and looked forward to seeing it on the houseboat. She was a bit surprised that it was hanging on a houseboat on a dock in Tennessee. JW had to assure her, it is not 'just a houseboat', you will be astounded when you see this place. She noticed Charlie's chest puff up slightly when she talked about his the boat. She was just the opposite and felt embarrassed when Leah bragged on her friend's success. They were very different, but she had always heard opposites attract and she certainly hoped so.

"Guys, I hate to be a party pooper, but I'm exhausted and we have a big day tomorrow, I need my beauty sleep?" JW said.

Charlie said, "No you really don't." as he rocked and exhaled a puff. "Can you sit with me a minute— just the two of us?" He cocked his head to one side as he asked the question.

God, this man makes me crazy, her heart was beating so fast, but she tried not to show it. Leah and Katie quickly uttered their good nights and disappeared inside. He patted his lap, and said would you come sit close so we can talk.

"I guess so." She put one arm around his neck, sat down in his lap, leaned back into his arms, and let him hold her. This was a new feeling for her, she had never been this exposed to a man in her life. It felt good, and she tingled all over, both of their breaths synchronized. She nuzzled her face into his neck

"M-m-m, you feel good," he said, "I could get used to this. You know I think I'm falling in love with you. I know it's early, but JW, I have loved you since the 8th grade. I was just too afraid to tell you. God, you didn't even know I was alive. I was such a scrawny jerk." He was playing with her hair as he talked in a low soft whisper. It happened just as it does in the movies, is all she thought. The next thing she knew his lips were on hers, and she felt the surge of adrenaline rush through her body, she felt the tingle in her toes. They were tangled up in one another's arms, the kiss started soft and slow, and she could feel his rough chin scratch her face. She didn't care. They could not pull apart, and she moved her hands to hold his face, she was not stopping him this time. He gently parted her lips with his tongue and put himself inside of her, vulnerable and sending the message, she longed to receive. She opened herself to him, and gently suckled. He groaned and she shuddered simultaneously. This was the way it was supposed to be, soft and gentle. She began gently biting his face, his neck, kissing his chest and his hands started to roam up her back to loosen her bra...then, the flashback came. She froze.

"Stop, no, don't," she yelled and stood up abruptly.

Charlie looked at her as if she had two heads, "What's wrong, I thought you wanted me to..."

She interrupted him, "Charlie, I can't do this, it's too soon, there are things you need to know and I can't talk about it with you right now, I'm just not ready. I need to go." She turned and ran to her room, gently crying. However, she didn't go to her room; she tapped on Leah's door.

"Sister, I need you, can I come in?" Leah opened the door. JW collapsed in her arms, "I need help."

# FOURTEEN

The next morning JW awoke in Leah's bed and found her sitting on the chaise in the sunlight streaming in through the open window. The birds outside were chirping loudly and the curtains danced in the soft summer breeze.

"I can see why you love this place," Leah said.

"I'm so sorry for last night, I just have trouble sometimes." She said.

"I know, sweetie, its ok. I have known you for a lotta years, I know all about your trouble. I am just happy to be here for you. You know, if you ever want to talk about these things, I will listen. I will never tell a soul. It may actually help you to talk about it."

JW knew her friend meant well, but she had no clue what she would be unleashing. Once you hear such things, they can't be unheard, and it was her nightmare.

"No, I'm fine, truly. Let's get ready; we have a big day ahead." JW said.

When she sheepishly saw Charlie in the dining room, he acted as if nothing had transpired the night before. That was fine with her too.

"Ok, guys, here's the plan," Charlie said, "I have to run to the office this morning and do some work, so let's take two vehicles. I'll meet you all on the square around 11, we'll look around, do lunch at some booths, listen to some great fiddlers, and then

I have to head back to the shop. Does that sound OK with you?"

Leah said to JW, "Maybe you can drive me out to the farm you just inherited, and show me around the town?"

JW shook her head and smiled, she was ashamed of her behavior from the evening before. Charlie was such a good man and he deserved better than her brokenness, she thought. I really wish I had never come back; it is stirring up too many bad memories.

A light breeze blew to keep things cool the sun was shining, and it was a perfect day for a festival in the South. The square was decked out regally from the leftover 4th of July decorations, with lots of red, white, and blue and flags draping the main building. JW did a report on the courthouse once in school, so she proceeded to tell Leah the history of the Courthouse Square Historic District. Listed on the National Register of Historic Places in the '80's, Leitchfield has become known as "The Fiddling Capital of Kentucky" due to the Twin Lakes National Fiddler Championship. The event held annually on the Court Square, brings thousands to hear the best musicians for near and far. Past champions have gone on to become well-known fiddle players for stars such as Faith Hill, Clint Black, Steve Wariner and many others.

JW remembered the Courthouse square because at one time, it housed the county jail too, and she had, on more than one occasion; accompanied Momma and Aunt Minnie down here in the middle of the night to secure bail for her wayward cousin.

Most people in town knew her as Luther's cousin, they had no clue she was a famous artist from New York now.

Today she was trying to see her hometown through new eyes, experience it just like Leah. She began to think maybe things had changed here; but soon found, it was not to be. They stood out like two sore thumbs in the crowd. She wanted Leah to enjoy her day and see the best of small town living. Instead, she experienced perhaps the worst.

They walked arm in arm, as old friends in the neighborhood in New York will do. JW had just bought a lemon shake-up from one of the food booths; this was her all-time favorite fair beverage. The shakeup recipe is huge amounts of pure white sugar, crushed ice and a little sour lemon juice shaken between two large plastic cups until it mixed into a sweet nectar of the Gods. It is not for everyone though. She had not had this drink since she had left home; so, she shared a sip from her cup with Leah. A bald headed man strode forcefully toward them; you could see the crowds parting in his wake. He wore black leather pants, biker boots, with a chain dangling off his belt and a do-rag tied around his forehead. He had on a T-shirt with the sleeves haphazardly cut out at the seams, exposing his large biceps, and a black leather vest with an assortment of patches sewn on. He looked as dirty as he smelled. As he got closer his pace slowed, that's when JW saw the tats. Swastikas were darkly etched in his arms, and on his scalp, at first JW paid him no mind. Then Leah grabbed her arm tighter and was shaking, as she whispered, "Look, he's coming at us!"

The man walked up to her and said, "We don't want no dyke's here, you all need to quit hanging off each other, go back where you belong."

Leah shot back in her regional New York rich Jewish accent, "hey, back off, get outta' here."

Once he heard Leah's accent, and saw the Star of David necklace she always wore, he had a completely new barrage of anti-Semitic epithets to hurl at them.

Where was Charlie, JW thought? If he saw or heard the commotion, he would help them, but help never arrived. Finally, the skinhead got tired of yelling at the immovable women, and he began to fire up the crowd around them. A few did join in and JW could tell Leah was mad and scared, but they both stood firm and tall and bravely held tightly on to each other.

Finally, JW had enough of his belligerent barrage, and said in the twang she had worked so hard to rid from her diction, "that's 'nuff, you stinkin' hillbilly. You need ta' get outta her and crawl back under th' rock you came from under and leave us be, before I have somebody come kick yur ass." Some in the crowd started to clap and whistle, and with the backing from the majority of the crowd, the man slinked off. He did give them the middle finger salute before he departed.

JW was afraid he would return with more supporters, so they walked calmly to their car and headed out of town, making sure no one was following. JW apologized profusely to her dear friend; she had never experienced this type of hatred before. Leah while shaken responded, "Oy Vey," followed with a slight pause and exhale, "shit happens," and they then laughed to lighten the mood.

What JW and Leah didn't know is that Charlie had seen the whole thing; he was coming around the corner of the building from parking his truck nearby, when he heard the commotion. He saw all of it, and he knew the biker skinhead, very well. Charlie made a conscious decision to stay out of it, he had defended JW once, and it almost cost him his career. He wasn't going to rescue her again, and she didn't need to know. He was not her savior he thought, as he turned and headed back to his truck and drove to the trucking company shop, cold and unfeeling with no remorse.

# FIFTEEN

After their harrowing day at the town square, JW drove Leah around the small town and out to see the farm. The car windows were down and they were enjoying nature and the wind in their hair. Since it was Shabbat, the Jewish Sabbath, and out of respect to Leah, JW would not turn on the radio or use her phone. The use of electronics was prohibited on the Sabbath. The Sabbath is a holy day, and to be observed as a day of rest and worship. So, she opted for a quick drive by the farm, and then they would return to rest at the B&B. The Shabbat would officially end at sundown, after three stars appeared in the night sky. Early the next morning they would head to the lake, Charlie had invited them for a cruise on the houseboat. After today's chaos, they looked forward to the tranquility of the soothing lake. She could hardly wait to tell Charlie about the excitement of today, but she wouldn't see him until morning.

Their day started bright and early, the three of them packed and headed to the lake. Charlie phoned ahead and had the dock stock the boat with food and supplies. JW could hardly wait to show Leah the lake and the opulent houseboat. It was beyond description.

Leah had an ulterior motive, which was to learn as much as she could about Charlie's past. Anything she found out she could tell the man Joseph hired to investigate Charlie. Joseph had been oddly quiet about the investigator. He had asked Leah to leave the details to him. He had family connections that would be very useful for something like this. It honored Joseph to help their dear friend, who he believed was his family too. He cautioned his love to be careful, their people's story had been one of strife for generations, and he knew too well the hatred harbored in men's hearts.

Leah enjoyed the ride through the countryside, and when the truck emerged from between the rocks to the view of the lake, she gasped as JW had. The first sight of the lake snaking around the bend will never grow old, JW thought. When they boarded the boat, Leah could not believe her eyes, the interior and square footage rivaled many of the Upper East Side penthouses she had been privy to visit. She now realized the painting did belong on this boat, and for once in her life, JW seemed deeply happy.

After the walk about the boat, Charlie captained to his favorite cove and tied off, followed by swimming, floating, drinks, perfectly grilled steaks, more drinks, and relaxing in the hot tub. JW had told Leah about their previous stargazing from the sky bridge, and she was excited to see for herself. The stars were so much brighter in the pitch-black night of the lake; in the city, the lights and buildings blocked the view of the twinkling universe. Of course, the romance and constellations drawn on the palm of her hand were missing; the night sky was nonetheless amazing. She even saw several shooting stars. It was as if they put on a show just for her.

Leah initiated small talk, "Charlie, I know nothing about you, tell me how all this is possible," and she waved her hands around as if she was conjuring the boat. "JW tells me you were in the military too?"

"Well, I was stupid enough to sign up while at A&M; I wanted to see the world and I did. Had boot camp was at Camp Lejeune, NC. There I became a Recon Marine. Our moto is, 'A Recon Marine can speak without saying a word and achieve what others can only imagine.' I had gruesome training for six months; it was hardest thing I have ever done. I died twice." He chuckled.

"Wow," Leah said, "I had no idea."

"They taught us survival, evasion, resistance, and escape, 'SERE' for short. Those bastards dropped me in the middle of the ocean and I had to find my bearings and swim out. Dumped me in the desert with a compass a knife and a bottle of water and I had to hike out. Then they dropped me in the swamp in Florida to fight out of, and the snow in Alaska, where I had to save myself." He said.

"But, I did it," he said proudly.

"I crossed the equator on the USS Blue Ridge as a pollywog and transitioned into a shellback, I am officially a Son of Neptune. I did a tour in Afghanistan," he sighed heavily. In the Corps I did some things I'm proud of, and some things I'm not so proud of." His voice trailed and he visibly winced at the memory, he let out a cleansing breath. "When I was done over there, I couldn't wait to get back here, and I'm not leaving of my own volition ever again." He said.

"I don't blame you," she said, "You have an amazing life here."

He had a little buzz going, and kept talking, Leah let him ramble, "That guy that you all tangled with on the square yesterday, he was in the Corps at one time," he scoffed, "I was surprised to see JW stand up to him like she did. The dude had some chemical dependency going on and couldn't cut it. That's probably why she was able to put him down like she did."

Leah flinched and quickly looked toward JW, "How did you know about the incident on the square? You weren't there, and I know Leah hasn't told you yet?"

Charlie realized what he had said too late, "I heard about it from one of the guys at the trucking company afterward. You know how word travels in a small town." He tried to sound convincing.

JW cast her eyes downward and pretended she didn't hear, but they both knew he was lying.

But why would he lie? Why would he watch the awfulness of what unfolded, and not intervene? She was not going to be alone with him tonight, she was afraid she couldn't stop herself again, and she was now beginning to be afraid of him. What else could he be lying about? Somethings not right here, she thought. She couldn't wait for this night to be over and for them to get out of town.

# SIXTEEN

The tension was palpable in the truck as the three of them drove back to the B&B. JW couldn't quite put her finger on the issue, but something didn't make sense to her, Leah was eerily quiet. Charlie seemed to be tense, his muscles in his face would clench, and release, he was not relaxed like he usually was when he returned from the restful lake. JW tried to make small talk, but to no avail, so she finally gave up, rested her head on the window, and immersed herself in her cell phone.

Upon arrival at the B&B, Katie said to JW, "Strange, but you have a letter in today's mail."

The letter was typed and addressed to Wanda Jane Walker, C/O Cooper Farms B&B, with no return address. "Who on earth would be sending me mail here—it must be from the attorney's office," she said. She ripped open the envelope and turned white, just letting the letter dangle in midair so Leah and Katie could both see at the same time. Typed in bold letters, 'GO HOME JEW LOVER BEFORE YOU DIE! I KNOW YOUR SECRETS. The note also had skulls, swastikas, and a knife with dried blood dripping off the bottom of the page. Well, this looks serious she thought, now what do we do?

Leah knew immediately what she was going to do. Pack her bags and head for the airport and she was taking JW with her. Anti-Semitism was nothing new to Leah, she had faced it most of her life. However, she and JW were alone and unprotected in this small southern town. Leah knew of the deep ties of the Ku Klux Klan—'KKK' or the Klan and the south, it was one of the reasons Joseph did not want her to come here alone.

While studying film history at Tisch, and D.W. Griffith's silent film, "Birth of a Nation," she learned the history of the Klan. There have actually been three distinct eras of the KKK's secret society in America's sordid past. The film mythologized and glorified the founding of the group, founded in Pulaski, Tennessee and began after the Civil War in 1865. The primary target was blacks however; they have since spread the hatred to Jews, immigrants, leftists, LGBT, Muslims, and Catholics. Their modus-operandi includes terrorism, physical assault, and even lynching. All three movements have called for the "purification" of American society. The second era of the Klan was founded atop Stone Mountain, Georgia in early 1900's and members donned white sheets, pointed caps, to hide their identities. They burned crosses and terrorized targets during night raids wounding and killing mostly blacks. The third rise of the Klan, began with the civil rights movement of the early 60's, and consisted of several organizations. These have evolved and begun to merge with other hate groups like the paramilitary and neo-Nazi organizations. Fast forward to 2020 and we have skinheads visiting small town fairs, probably trying to recruit new blood. One of these organizations, The Imperial Klan's of America

(IKA), was founded in 1996 in Dawson Springs, Kentucky is a mere 86 miles from Leitchfield. That was too close for comfort for Leah and Joseph.

JW and Leah wasted no time in packing their bags and heading to Louisville. Flights were booked in route, no expense barred; their number one objective was to get out of town—fast. They arrived at LaGuardia later that night.

Charlie began calling JW's cell before the plane sat down on the tarmac, and he left numerous messages for JW. His tone fraught with concerned. When JW retrieved the voice mail, she had a decision to make. Do I call him back? Was there a future there and I'm running away again? What should I do?

Leah was no help in this decision, she said to JW, "Schatzi, you need to follow your heart, this is your decision."

JW decided there was no rush. I'll call him tomorrow, I've had enough drama for one day. She also planned to work in the studio, which was in the back of Leah and Joseph's art gallery. The setup made it easy for her to create large pieces without risk of damage. She could prepare and hang them in the gallery with less cost, no need to crate, and better security. She needed to loose herself in her art for a while.

Early the next day in the studio, she was engrossed in her oils, had her Alexa blaring music when the delivery bell rang. The man carried into the room the largest bouquet of long-stem red roses and baby's breath she had ever seen. There had to be four dozen roses in the massive arrangement tied with a wide red

satin bow. A note attached to the ribbon scripted in
calligraphy, read:

## The Dancer in Red

*I saw her in the garden, watched her dance in the gentle
wind,
I walked by with a watchful eye, and prayed to see her
again;*

*Like a little dancer on a music box, she twirled all
around,
I admired her from afar, and never made a sound.*

*There she was before me, dressed in radiant red,
I slowly walked up to her—not remembering what I said.*

*I gently pulled her close to me and smelled her sweet
perfume,
I was lost in time and space, on a warm summer noon.*

*I touched her lips of ruby red—closed my eyes and drifted
away.
I will think of her often, and always remember that day.*

*The leaves are turning color-yellow, red and brown,
Twirling like little dancers as they go round and down.*

*She will be leaving me, so sad to see her go,
She will return—in the spring, after the winter's snow.*

*My lovely "Red Rose," she will grow and bloom in the
month of June,*

*When I will once again, touch her ruby red lips*
*and smell her sweet perfume.*

Each time I look at the painting on the boat, I dream of you.

Please don't make me wait til spring to feel you, to smell you, to love you.

Please come back to me.
I love you,
Charlie

First, she cried, and then she picked up the phone and called Charlie.

"I got the flowers, and the poetry. Did you write this for me?"

"Who else? How soon can you come back to me, I'll protect you and keep you safe. Please don't leave me like this; I think we have something—something real. Don't run away from me.," he said pleadingly.

She could feel the pain in his voice, which made her long to hold him and kiss his lips. They definitely had chemistry, and she thought what if he is my 'bashert' and I miss my chance? She said, "I have some work I have to finish here, but I'll get a flight for next week. Tell Katie to have my room ready."

"Hurry, I am lost without you my love. I will call you every night and we can look at the stars together," he said.

# SEVENTEEN

Before JW returned to Leitchfield to spend more time getting to know Charlie, Leah and Joseph asked her to come for supper and to meet someone. Leah was very secretive about the invitation and her other guest. She would not divulge much information, very unlike Leah.

"It will become clear as glass to you, when you arrive," she said.

When JW arrived, Leah greeted her warmly, "my sweet, we have some exciting news to share with you," as JW walked into the living room she saw the other guest. It was a man about her age, and he had a very dark countenance, and very reserved and confident. He was sitting on the sofa, and he politely stood when she entered the room. He appeared dark in all ways, his attire, his features, his deep brown eyes—with the longest and darkest lashes, and his hair shorn very close to his head and a rugged five-o'clock shadow. He wore a custom yarmulke. You could tell that if he let his hair grow longer, the curls would be enviable of most women. He was very fit and his clothing clung tightly to his tall, slim, and yet muscular frame. She extended her hand to him, and he smiled at her, not a fake one, but a real smile that included the eyes. He had a very bright and white smile with perfect teeth. He clasped her hands warmly, and bowed slightly at the waist as he said softly, "Hello, I am Eli Cohen." He had a slight Yiddish accent, and his speech had the same cadence of Leah and Joseph, the way he spoke rang familiar to her. She noticed he wore no wedding ring.

Leah said, "Come, let us eat while the meal is hot, we can talk afterwards."

The meal was typically Jewish and fully kosher; Leah started serving chicken soup, roasted chicken and potato latkes. The dessert was a handmade Mandelbrot, which are Jewish biscotti. Leah prepared hot tea to dip the cookies into; she had outdone herself on the dinner. It was delicious and prepared with love.

Joseph stood and started talking seriously to her, "JW, my friend Eli is also my cousin, and he is the man that will be looking into Charlie Cooper for you. He comes by way of an organization that my family has befriended for many years. What I am about to share with you cannot leave this room. Is that understood?"

"I guess, why all the drama Joseph? You're scaring me."

"Well my darling, with what we are dealing, you perhaps should be scared." Joseph's voice trailed solemnly.

Joseph proceeded to tell JW that his family, which holds dual citizenship, as Israeli-Americans are known as 'Sayanims.' This is a Hebrew word, a Sayan is a helper; we provide logistical support like shelter, and money to the Israeli intelligence. These are many Sayanims around the world, we happen to be in New York City. An example, he explained, if you own a rental car agency, you assist someone such as Eli rent a car without all the legal paperwork so that cannot be traced.

He said, "Eli is a special collections officer. Do you understand what I am telling you? He is a specialist from Israel that will help us."

She blinked, "What do you mean? Why do you think we need someone like this to look at Charlie?"

"We may not, but this organization is setup to help Jews around the world. As faithful Sayan, we are due a favor. Eli has many research tools at his disposal and this help is a gift to you little sister," he said.

Eli sensed JW's concern about the cloak and dagger approach. He wanted to alleviate her fears.

He looked at JW and spoke, "I will do my work under cover, and you will not even know that I am around. Most of which will be done behind the scenes at the office, I may require a visit to Kentucky, but it will be with the aid of Sayan's and go unnoticed, if I am blessed."

"So, I just go about my life as usual, when will you let me know what you know?" She asked.

"I am not sure at this time; I wanted to meet you before we began our work. To see with my own eyes what your reaction would be, I am satisfied. I am now ready to begin immediately, I would be delighted to help the sister of my cousin," and Eli giggled a bit when he said this. "Enough of this business talk let us get to know one another."

The rest of the evening was delightful; she enjoyed learning more about Joseph's family that remained in

Israel. They spoke of aunts, uncles, and cousins remaining in Tel Aviv. Joseph went down memory lane talking of the many dinners and family get together's they shared in the back yards of their grandparents' home in Israel. Sharing stories of the olive trees in the back yard and the harvest in the fall when the fruit was ripe. The deep family history and love of their country made her long for a link to descendants like those they shared.

Eli also shared fascinating stories of travelling the world, and marvelous sights he has seen. His smile was easy, and his demeanor was kind and gentle—this person is probably a desk jockey and they are trying to make him out like 007. She smiled at the thought, and felt this was over reacting by Joseph and Leah, and perhaps they were trying to impress Joseph's cousin too. However, it made her love them more, if possible, for their concern for her future. She also believed this would give her and Charlie a great story to share in their old age, when they told their love story to their kids and grandkids.

At the end of the night, they agreed that she would go back to the Cooper B&B and act as if nothing was up. Eli, through Leah, would let her know when they had the dossier on Charlie prepared. He worked fast, so within two weeks it should be resolved. She hoped during that time she would also know whether what she and Charlie had was real, but she needed to slow things down with him. She was not ready for a physical relationship and she needed to let him know. She also had a very difficult conversation they would need to have before this went much farther. The disturbing revelation may drive him away before Eli even gets his report completed.

Eli suggested he walk JW back to her apartment, and she gladly took him up on the offer. She was so relaxed and pleased to continue their interesting conversation of their different worlds and the couple that had brought them together. Eli did not have an apartment in New York, but relied upon relatives and sayanims for lodging when he was in town, and now he was staying with Joseph. He traveled frequently in his job, he didn't talk much about what he actually did for a living, and he didn't act as if he wanted to either. So, she let it be.

As they walked down the New York sidewalk in the dark night, which at times could be very frightening, for once she felt very calm. For once in her life, her guard was completely down, she felt safe beside Eli, and that did not happen often.

She didn't want the night to end, but they reached her apartment door.

"Eli, would you like to come in for a nightcap?"

"My dear, we are not permitted to be alone together. The only way for that to happen is to leave your door open, and I don't think that is a good idea," he said with a chuckle.

"Oh, sorry, I'll say goodnight then, hope to see you again," she extended her hand and he took it in and seemed to hold on for a little longer than usual.

"Until we meet again, Shalom," and he was gone.

# EIGHTEEN

JW arrived at the B&B the following week and Charlie was waiting for her on the porch as she pulled into the drive. He started walking toward the driveway when he saw the car turn off the main road.

"Hello beautiful, I am so glad to see you," as he put his arms around her, pulling her into him, and kissing her on the lips. "U-m-m-m you feel so good,"

She was ambivalent about being back in this place, the source of so much pain and yet, possibly her future home.

He said, "I hope you're up to some excitement tonight, I have a bunch of friends getting together for some drinks, and who knows what? Are you up for it?"

"Sure, it would be great to meet your friends." She meant that too, it would help her to see where she might fit in and how he acts in a familiar environment. "When and where?" She asked.

"How 'bout you go freshen up, and I'll be back to pick you up at 7. We'll grab a bite, and then meet the gang at the watering hole around 9." He said.

He carried her bags to the room, and left her with a lingering kiss at the door before saying goodbye for a few hours. She was genuinely happy to be there, and she tried not to think about Eli lurking around watching them.

Promptly at seven, he pulled into the drive, and

JW was on the porch waiting. Charlie hopped energetically out of the truck and her heart jumped a beat when she saw him. He was dressed all in black. He wore skintight black jeans, which showed every bulge, with a large silver belt buckle. He had black cowboy boots with silver tips, a black t-shirt, and a black suede cowboy hat. The t-shirt fit him snugly and accentuated his pectoral muscles. She could see his Marine tatts on his arms, and she thought she could make out the six-pack hiding beneath, or it could have been her imaginative thinking.

"Hey cowboy, wanna take me for a ride?" She said, and then felt stupid.

"I sure do," he flashed his pearly white teeth and held out his hand for hers, just like prince charming.

After dinner, they went to a local bar, called "The Watering Hole," which JW though amusing. As soon as Charlie walked in behind her, she heard in unison a group yelling, "Charlie!" He raised his hat and guided her to a back room, there were about ten people already well on their way to an alcohol buzz. She smiled, and thought, oh boy, I hope these people like me, and I like them.

Charlie said, "Guys, this is my friend from New York, JW. JW this is the guys, he proceeded to introduce each of them but she tuned out the names. Her ears perked when he said one she recognized. "This is Brenda Johnson." It can't be the Brenda from high school that we knew as a cheerleader, and the same Brenda that broke Charlie's heart by cheating on him with a football player?

JW said, "Brenda Johnson, did we go to school

together with Charlie, that Brenda Johnson?"

She said, "Yes," sheepishly and not questioning JW on how she would know that.

JW never told the group that she was a native of the town and she never told Brenda Johnson who she was either. For some strange reason, she didn't think she needed to—she thought to herself, she already knows who I am. Why, how could she? The rest of the night, she was observing more that interacting, she wondered what was going on and why would Brenda be in Charlies circle of friends. Something is rotten in Denmark, she thought to herself.

What she noticed throughout the night, especially as the beer and drinks flowed, was that everywhere Charlie was Brenda was nearby. JW excused herself to the ladies room; Brenda was standing at the pub table right next to Charlie and leaning over his chair arm with her ample bosom near his face, when she came back. Her top had been unbuttoned even more than when the evening started, JW was sure of this. Every time Charlie touched JW's arm or gently swiped an errant hair dangling from her face, she saw a flash of anger in Brenda's eyes.

Suddenly, it dawned on her; she is in love with Charlie. Then her mind started racing, does he know about Brenda's feelings? Has he been with her and I am now an unwitting participant in a love triangle? She suddenly had more questions than answers. How does she know my identity, and who told her? The only people that know me, she thought, are Charlie, Katie, Luther, and the Attorney. She immediately ruled out Katie and the Attorney, which left Charlie and Luther. Clearly Brenda the school bus driver and cousin Luther do not run in the same circles, so that leaves one suspect standing—Charlie.

JW decided to play it cool, don't jump to conclusions prematurely, she told herself. Give this man a chance to explain, maybe it's innocent. After all, Brenda looks like she has had a big fall from popular high school cheerleader to a mimpy divorcee. Nevertheless, she was anxious for this gathering to end.

About midnight, Charlie had enough and asks her by snuggling into her ear, "are you ready to blow this joint?"

"More than ready," she said.

They were the first to leave the party of small town drunks, in a small town bar, in a small town. JW had nursed one beer for the night, while Charlie had not. She took his keys without objection and found her way through the dark night back to the B&B, and he dozed. She helped Charlie navigate the stairs and deposited him in the vacant room across the hall, clothes, and all. She tiptoed to her room and securely locked the deadbolt, just in case he sleepwalks and gets lost, she thought.

She had many questions, for a sober Charlie and wished it weren't so late so she could call Leah and tell her all about this weird evening. She decided she would withhold some of the character damaging details, for she did not want Leah to think badly of Charlie. After all, she thought, everybody drinks one to many sometimes, right? Well—Joseph didn't, she thought, but he was an enigma, you couldn't compare anyone to Joseph.

With that thought, she turned out the lights, tossed, and turned fitfully. In the middle of the night, around 3 a.m. she awoke when she heard Charlie's truck engine start. The lights shone on her bedroom curtains when the truck roared to life. The wheels crunched on the gravel of the driveway, as it slowly crept down the long drive. She peaked out the window and heard it accelerate, and watched as it turned onto the highway back towards town. She was puzzled, and wondered where or whom Charlie was going to visit at this hour?

# NINETEEN

The next morning, JW was up early and decided to run to town for a bite at the local truck stop. She had heard that they had a killer breakfast of bacon, eggs, biscuits, gravy, grits, and hotcakes if you wanted them, and she wanted them. She had not eaten like this since she last sat at her momma's breakfast table; she wanted to revisit that pleasant memory.

The restaurant was located in a truck stop off the interstate that sold diesel fuel, and had been around for as long as she could remember. The facility was for long-haul truckers and had restroom and showers, laundro-mat, snacks, and a diner serving hot meals. It was the quintessential greasy spoon menu. There were three rows of tables in room, about 12 tables in all. Covering each table was a red and white checked vinyl tablecloth. Benches sat facing each other on each side of the table, which could seat two comfortably. The benches were covered with solid red vinyl and had seen better days, many of the benches, had holes in the vinyl, exposing cotton batting or raw wood. There was a long counter nearest the kitchen, which had the cash register on one end, with bar stools running the length. The floor was tile and it was sticky from a light greasy film. There weren't many customers in the diner at this time of day; the truckers were there early in the morning or late in the evening. An old man and woman sat by the window nearest the front door, not talking to one another. His face buried in a newspaper and she drank coffee and staring out the window into the pot-holed parking lot

"I'll have coffee black, stack of hotcakes, and the number two—scrambled," she said to the server. JW took out her cell phone and checked messages and emails, as usual nothing there. She planned to call Leah, after she got back to the B&B from breakfast and fill her in on bits and pieces of last night's adventure.

She had stuffed her face with as much as she could hold, and had finished her second cup of strong black coffee, when the door opened. She looked up and in walked her worst nightmare, He staggered in through the doorway and fell around the room, probably coming off an all-nighter, and then he saw her. He headed straight for her table. She looked around to see if there was anyone to help her if need be, she grabbed her phone and immediately dialed 91 and held her finger poised over the last digit ready in case she needed help. Luther slid onto the bench seat across from her.

"Well, well, ifn' it ain't my dear cuz," he sneered, smelling of alcohol with missing front teeth and stinking smoke breath.

"What do you want? Are you stalking me?" She said firmly and unafraid, while inside she was trembling.

"Now cuz, don't go using that type of talk, you'll get me in trouble with the law," he laughed as he talked. "I want what's mine. That land belongs to me;

I lived there with that old mean witch for all those years. I deserve it," he said. He reached over the table and grabbed her wrist tightly, she winced and tried to pull back spilling her coffee.

"Let go of me," she said loudly. The two old heads turned to look toward their table, but no one would go up against this angry man to help her. She knew she was on her own, as usual.

"I am not the scared little girl you once threatened and hurt. I was nine years old when you did what you did to me. You destroyed my life, my innocence, you robbed me," trying to wrench free. "You are an animal, and I am not afraid of you anymore. They should lock you up and throw away the key for what you did to me. You won't scare me into silence again," she seethed with anger and shook with emotion as she spoke through gritted teeth.

"Looky who's got all big and brave after all these years? Awe honey, it was good for me, wasn't it good for you?" He laughed crazily. Then he pulled her even more tightly and said, "You better be afraid of me, you fuckin' bitch. You think I hurt you once, that ain't nothing compared to what I'm gonna do to you. That sweet little ass of your is all I've been thinking about since I saw you in that lawyer's office. It's gonna be fun, you should enjoy it." He stood up and pulled her to her feet, knocking over their benches with a loud noise.

She was terrified and she knew if he got her out of this place, no one would ever find her body. Unsure of what to do, she was looking for a weapon—anything she could use to fight him.

Unnoticed she slipped a butter knife into her coat pocket as he jerked her up from the table, she was not going down without a fight and she vowed to give him one.

She said, "Luther, I am not going anywhere with you, let go of my arm, NOW!"

He grabbed her more tightly and pulled her to his chest, "Shut-up, you fuckin' bitch," as he slapped her hard across the face.

Bleeding from her nose, he jerked her toward the door, she skidded her feet on the tile floor trying to slow him down, but he was much stronger. Her mind was panicking, what to do, what to do? I'll just fall down she thought, she had learned in a self-defense classes that dead weight was hard to lift. She also learned, never get in the car with an abductor willingly. When they got outside, she dropped suddenly onto the pavement and curled her body into the fetal position, wrapping her arms around her face and pulling her knees to her chest. At the very moment, a black flash appeared in her peripheral vision out of nowhere, and she saw a foot land in Luther's chest. He fell back towards the car, cursing. He pulled a knife from his pocket, but a whir of hands and feet flew through the air and the knife jettisoned across the parking lot. JW was afraid to move, she was afraid to open her eyes more than a slit, to see who was trying to go up against evil Luther. She heard flesh slap flesh, bones crunch, and a car horn started blaring. She knew Luther would hurt or kill anyone that had been brave enough to help her, and after the silence, she expected him to start dragging her on to the car to her death. She then heard, feet running and a car screeching out of the parking lot and hands on her again. She fought the hands, slapping and stammering, 'No, No, No." …..but a calm voice whispering in Yiddish she heard, "fradyndine, my friend, it is I Eli, you are safe now, let us go." He lifted her effortlessly to her feet from the ground. When she stood, she realized she hurt her hip when she had dropped to the pavement. Limping and defeated, she leaned all of herself into him as he helped her get to her car.

"Where did you come from?" Her voice broke with sobs, "Thank God you were here," she cried into his chest. He softly patted her head with one hand and held her other hand tightly against himself.

He said with his accent, "It is all ok now, when you are composed we can talk about these things. Are you OK to drive?"

She nodded yes and she was incredulous that he spoke as if it was the most natural thing in the world to risk his life for her. Who was this brave man, she wondered? Maybe he really a 007, I cannot wait to call Leah.

# TWENTY

She softly cried all the way back to the B&B, and thought to herself, what if Eli had not been nearby. She would be dead, or worse, no doubt about it. What was she going to do about Luther the next time; he would not give up that easily.

When she walked in the door, Katie screamed, "Oh my God, JW, what happened to you? You're bruised and blood…" her voice trailed off as she ran to JW. ""Charlie is gonna kick some ass when he hears about this," she said.

"It's nothing, I was just in the wrong place at the wrong time," she said. "Katie, please don't say anything to Charlie, the last thing I need is to get him caught up in something he has no business getting into," she shook her head, stifled a whimper, and limped toward her room. "I'm gonna take a nice long hot bath and lay down for a while. I'll see you later, OK."

"I'm gonna tell him, no way am I keeping this from Charlie. I don't want him pissed at me," Katie said.

That is just great, JW thought to herself. Now, I have to explain this to Charlie, he's gonna ask a lot of questions. He's going to find out about my past, I'm damaged goods, why would even want me anymore. I am so ashamed; I knew I should have let Wanda stay dead and never come back to this God forsaken town. It's been nothing but trouble ever since I showed up at this place. She cried harder at the thoughts.

Just then her cell phone rang, Leah was calling, all I need right now.

"Hello," she said while wincing from the pain caused by her swollen and bloody lip. She looked into the mirror hanging over the dresser, taking a critical look. Yep, she thought, I look like shit. I wonder what Luther looks like. I heard some serious bone breakage back in that parking lot and she couldn't help but smile gingerly.

"JW, I got a call from Eli, how bad is it? Are you ok?" without waiting for an answer she kept asking, "Do you need me to come down there?"

"I'm fine, thanks to Eli. That guy is awesome, of course, you probably knew that," she said. "My pride is hurt worse than anything." She went on to explain exactly what happened, and about her feeble attempt to put a butter knife in her pocket, which she whipped out as she was talking to Leah. Raising it into the air and viewing herself in the mirror, she chuckled into the phone. She said, "I'm one bad Mother F'er," she and Leah burst into laughter at the same time.

Leah always knows how to calm me down and lift me up at the same time. She's another person I don't know what I'd do, without them being in my wheelhouse.

"Leah, you should have seen Eli fight. I couldn't see everything, because I was lying in the fetal position, and scared shitless. But, what I saw was not an office worker that uses technology all day. This dude was landing foot kicks, and breaking bones with his hands. He disarmed Luther who had a hunting knife and knows how to use it," she said. "Just who is this Eli Cohen anyway?

Leah proceeded to tell JW the full story of Eli. He was in fact a cousin of Joseph's from Israel. However, she elaborated Eli is with Israeli intelligence—The Mossad, but he is not an office worker. The Mossad is the Central Institute for Intelligence, and Special Operations. This group is responsible for intelligence collection, covert operations, and counter-terrorism around the world. She went on to explain, you remember the Munich Massacre in the Olympics in '72 by the Palestinian terrorist group, "Black September." She went on, afterward Golda Meir hired a group of Mossad Agents to track down and kill the Black September assassins. The Mossad's reputation is the most efficient secret killing machine in the world. Their motto" "By way of deception thou shalt make war." Eli trained in Israel for three years for his duties, and he is with the Metsada Special Operations Division. Their missions conduct highly sensitive assassination, sabotage, paramilitary, and psychological warfare projects.

"That sure as hell, explains a lot," she said. "Thank you and Joseph for looking out for me."

"Unfortunately," she said, "I've got some bad news too."

"What else could go wrong today?" JW asked.

"I hate to add to your problems, but, we received

a letter at the gallery today," she said.

"Oh, what prey tell?" She said sarcastically.

"It was a threatening letter, said something like you were a phony and a fraud, and that if we continued to represent and sell your art that they would expose you to the world. It said that you had an unsavory past that they would reveal to the world, great stuff. They want you out of Kentucky and to never come back," Leah said as if it was a joke.

"Oh, Leah, my career, everything I have worked for will be ruined," she cried. "I am a phony, I am not JW DuValle, and you know I reinvented myself when I left here. I do have a bad past, things I cannot even talk about with a secret that would destroy me, in many ways if people knew them. Charlie is here, what if we have a future together, I may be falling in love with this man," she confessed. "This has been the absolute worse day of my life to date, and that says a lot because I have had a pretty lousy life." She sighed heavily into the phone, as if she was about to give up.

"JW, listen to me, get a grip. This is nothing for you; look at how far you have come in life. You, my dear, are a fighter—even if it is with a butter knife," she laughed. "You just need to arm yourself and fight, do not give up so easily, especially if you are fighting for your bashert."

"I'm just so battered right now, I can't even think without crying, I need to lay down for a while," she said.

They said their good byes, she ran a hot bath, and tried to soak away her cares and troubles of the day.

Afterwards she planned a nap, and then she knew she would have to face Charlie. How would that go, and what would she be able to tell him....maybe something will come to me in my dreams. My career is in jeopardy, my face looks like hamburger, and the man I may love will soon know I am damaged goods.

What a hella day, she thought, "I'm going to bed."

# TWENTY-ONE

Eli was born in Tel Aviv, Israel as the fifth and last child and only son of Yosef and Sarah Cohen. He had served as most young men to, in the Israeli army. Afterwards he attended university, and studied abroad for a year.

Upon graduation, the Mossad recruited him into Israel's National Intelligence Agency and trained for a period of three years. Training consisted of foreign counter-intelligence, defensive driving, foot surveillance, and killing. Recognized for their hand-to-hand combat skills, the military self-defense and fighting system taught, was the Krav Maga, or contact combat. This technique derived from a combination of sources from aikido, boxing, wrestling, judo, and karate, and was deadly.

Eli passed all training programs with excellence and completed assignments around the world since his activation, most recently in New York City. There he rekindled the relationship with his cousin Joseph and his family. They had been very close as children visiting between summer vacations in Tel Aviv and New York City.

Eli's specialties were gathering information through hostage taking and interrogation. He found those skills to be of particular benefit in the small town where he was to gather information on target

Charlie Cooper.

Eli had been able to complete a biography easily since Charlie's service records were obtainable from Mossad computer systems, and cashing in a few favors. There were quite a few surprises in Charlie's records, which merited extreme diligence on his part. He needed to determine what Mr. Cooper had been up to since departure from the Marine Corps. This file also identified him as an extremely dangerous man. However, after observing Charlie undetected for a few days to understand his movements, Eli realized he would need to deploy additional skills to learn more.

He identified an associate to interrogate for the needed intel. The unlucky subject was a bigoted, neo-Nazi skinhead, and local drug user. He also happened to be the very man that had accosted Leah and JW on the city square a few weeks before. This was not by coincidence.

Eli determined the man to be a valuable resource when he tailed Charlie from the B&B one night at 3 a.m. and saw them meeting together in the trucking company parking lot. Eli observed, and photographed Charlie passing several duffle bags unloaded from a trailer backed into a bay. Eli needed to know what was in those bags. Where they originated, where they were going, and what was Charlie's involvement. If Eli were police, FBI, or DEA agent, he would have to employ different tactics; however, he had no constraints.

Under cover of darkness, Eli watched the transaction and followed the man and the merchandise as it moved to another dilapidated house on the run-down side of town. There were several motorcycles parked outside the house, and a confederate flag hung over the front window. He determined he would interrogate the man and release him if he cooperated, if not, he would do what was necessary.

The interrogation suite was an empty storage locker he had compromised on the outskirts of town. His only requirements were very little traffic, electricity and a door. Eli brought the other necessities with him. The capture was easy, since the man was in poor physical shape due to drink and drug use.

Eli grabbed him without witnesses as he left the flophouse late the next evening walking toward a dive bar down the road. He pulled his car over and called, when he came near, Eli clocked him with the butt of his gun, knocking him unconscious.

The skinhead woke up naked and zip-tied to a wooden armchair, with duct tape over his mouth, encircling his head. A bare light bulb hung very low over him.

The first thing Eli did was rip the tape off his mouth, calling him 'Nazi', because of all the swastika tattoos. While tied to a chair in the center of the storage locker, Eli tried to persuade him to talk.

"Make this easy on yourself 'Nazi', all I want is information; no one would know you ratted. Cooperate and it will be easier for both of us."

He paused for a few seconds, and said, "'Nazi', I really don't enjoy inflicting pain, but I am very good at it. Trust me. You don't want me to prove this to you."

The 'Nazi' spewed a barrage of curse words at Eli, with hatred. This was not a smart move, especially when hog-tied naked to a chair. However, the 'Nazi' was clearly not smart. He needed more persuasion.

Eli then brought the methods up to 'enhanced interrogation techniques'. He placed a black hood over 'Nazi's' head, and started high decibel heavy metal rock music on a repeat loop. Eli prepared a cross beam suspended from a rafter in the shed and handcuffed a naked, and hooded 'Nazi' standing on his tiptoes to the torture device. Then he left him to bake in this position overnight.

When Eli returned to the shed the next night, he found the 'Nazi' almost done.

"'Nazi', are you ready to talk to me?"

Still, no, Eli determined that this man was more afraid of Charlie and the people he worked for than he was of Eli. Eli intensified the interrogation.

He fastened the wooden chair to a long, wide board reclining at a 20-degree angle and secured it to the wall. 'Nazi' was let down from the cross-hanger and tied into the chair again. Eli removed the hood, terror and wild white eyes showed on the 'Nazi's' face. He was close to talking, Eli thought. He placed a wet cloth over 'Nazi's' face and with a bottle of water he began to drop a steady light stream of water over his nose and mouth. This caused the man to experience a drowning sensation and immediately the 'Nazi' began to gag and couldn't breathe through the wet cloth, air flow was restricted. 'Nazi' was ready to talk in 14 seconds. Eli stopped the waterboarding, removed the cloth, and they had a long discussion.

Now, what to do with 'Nazi', wondered Eli? He did not like to dispatch targets unless necessary, this man did not know nor would he ever see Eli again. The decision was made to deposit him within a block of the house where the Confederate flag hung, but not before encouraging him to find another line of work. The one he was in was not healthy for him, 'Nazi' agreed.

After the interrogation, Eli's assignment was complete. He had the report finalized on Charlie Cooper and was ready to deliver it to Joseph. However, since JW was staying at the B&B longer, he needed to stay near her. Her life may well be in danger, from the man that attacked her in the truck stop. She was vulnerable and Eli felt a connection to her that he had not felt before. He could not abandon her without protection until she knew what she was getting herself into with Charlie Cooper.

# TWENTY-TWO

Katie punched Charlie's number from her cell phone, he answered on the first ring.

"What's up sis, you never call me when I'm working," he said with a smile.

"Oh my God, Charlie, you should see JW. She just got the shit beat out of her. She came in crying and had a bloody and bruised face. I think you need to get over here, she needs you," Katie said.

"On my way," she heard the car start up as he disconnected the phone. Within 15 minutes, the time it took to speed from the trucking company to her door he was there. "Where is she," as he ran in.

"Calm down big brother, she went to take a bath and clean up and said she might lay down for a minute."

"How bad is she? Katie, talk to me," she heard the Marine in his voice.

She knew this was the Recon Marine Charlie wanting a status update and he was in full attack mode. She needed to try to settle him down before something bad happened.

"Charlie, let me make you a cup of coffee, and sit for a minute while she pulls herself together. She wouldn't want you to see her like she came in that door, trust me on this one," Katie said.

"Yeah, you're probably right about that, 'k give me a cup."

They sat in the kitchen around the familiar kitchen table and she stroked his hand, and spoke softly, to help him come down from the adrenaline high. His hands were rough from the fieldwork. Sadness overcame her suddenly for Charlie, she saw him in a new light. This tender and emotional man was a new side she rarely got to see. He had tried so hard to be the man and son that daddy always wanted, and daddy wanted a hard an unfeeling working farm hand. Daddy did not approve of the sensitive Charlie, so Charlie made him disappear. It made her sad that he had to hide himself from the world.

"Ok Katie, I'm calm, she's had time to clean up, I'm going back there and find out who did what, and then I'm going to go kill somebody today," Charlie said.

"Charlie, just go slow and easy, she's traumatized, I saw it in her eyes," Katie whispered.

At that, Charlie got up and strode down the hallway to the guest room. When he reached the door, he paused outside and placed his ear on the wooden door to see if he could hear her stirring or crying. His heart was pounding and his hair felt like it was physically standing upright. He tapped lightly as he said, "Baby, you in there? Are you Ok? Let me in, let me see you."

The door cracked open slightly and he could see only a small sliver of her face, it was unmarred. "Baby, you ok, open the door, c'mon," he said.

"I'm good Charlie, I don't need you to get involved in this, and it's a family thing. I'm ok."

"I know that's not true, open the door…..now,"

his tone changed to a command, not a sweet request.

She did as he said, she couldn't take much more today.

He took one look at her swollen and bruised lip and the beginning of a shiner and said, "Oh, baby, who did this to you?" He gently cupped her face with one hand while pulling her to him with the other and softly said, "Tell me about it."

She started sobbing uncontrollably, and let herself fall into his arms. It felt good to have someone to hold you, someone that would defend and protect her. She had never experienced this before, and she had never been bitch slapped either. She told Charlie all about her day and the chance run-in with Luther at the truck stop. She was so scared of him and what he was capable of and what he threatened to do to her. She knew he would too, if he got the chance. She could never be safe here, as long as he was around, she cried harder into Charlie's chest at the thought of being forced to flee again.

"JW, you are safe now, and you will be safe in the future, I will not let that piece of trash get near you again. You hear me good, he's never going to hurt you again," Charlie said.

"The last thing I need is for you to get into trouble with the law over that man, Charlie please do not go near him, promise me," she cried.

"Babe, you know I can't do that." He held her tightly, led her to the bed, and sat down with her just holding her next to him, sobbing into his chest. His heart was silently breaking, as he comforted her. He would rectify this situation soon, this will never happen again on my watch.

"Let me go get you an ice pack for that lip, it will help," Charlie said and he walked down the hallway toward Katie. "Can you take her an ice pack and maybe some Tylenol, unless you've got something stronger? I will be back in a little while, promise me you will take care of her. I've got to go see a man about a horse."

Uh-oh Katie thought, that is Charlies code word for the shit's gonna hit the fan, I would hate to be the dude that beat on his girl tonight.

"Sure brother, I'll take care of her. But, please don't get into trouble, I need you," she said

With that promise, he went to his bedroom, pulled out the footlocker from under his bed and flipped opened the box. He knew that this was like opening Pandora's Box. He anticipated what was inside, as if it were Christmas. Inside was a beautiful assortment of weapons, in ready to use condition. He picked up the 9mm Glock 19 sidearm like the one issued in the Corps. This one had served him well doing contract work. He wore it inside his waistline in a custom Kydex holder. It was very concealing but fast. In his shoulder holster, he had a 22lr Sig Sauer mosquito with a can suppressor using sub sonic ammo. The will work for the up and dirty work and was quiet. He pulled the Glock, disengaged the safety, and pulled back the slide in one fluid movement to release and chamber a round. He pressed the button on the side of the handgrip to eject the magazine. He verified the magazine was fully loaded, and re-inserted it by moving it briskly and firmly upward until it clicked. The gear reminded him of a warrior dressing to go into battle. He pulled two extra fully loaded 15 round magazines and stuffed them into his pockets, and placed the Glock back into the holster. In the locker were USMC issued black zip ties, and he had a new roll of duct tape. He found his Marine Recon issued, giant saw back Bowie knife, and he pulled it from the sheath and tested the blade. It was still as sharp and menacing as ever, the knife was over 16" long and could evoke fear in assailant's eyes. It could also fell a tree if necessary. He attached the sheath to his belt and slid the knife in and out a few times, to prime his muscle memory. After he was armed, he put on his black leather jacket to conceal his gear, his black nylon gloves, and black wraparound Oakley shades. He was ready to do battle. Now, he thought, let's go find this rat bastard. I have a score to settle.

# TWENTY-THREE

Luther cradling his left arm somehow lumbered to his pickup truck, and sped away. He knew his arm was broken, because it was quivering as it ached and bent grotesquely where it was supposed to be straight.

Who was that guy, he thought. Shit man, I never expected that to happen. I thought I had that bitch and could finish her for good. Well, it won't happen again, next time I'll just waste her on the spot with no witnesses. His addled brain thought, I'm her only living relative so if I play my cards right I'll get that land after all. If I don't, at least she won't live to have it either. She thinks she's so much better than me, and she always has, hatred, drug, and alcohol poisoned his mind.

Luther drove carefully, so not to attract unwanted attention from the police, toward the dilapidated house on the edge of town. It was a shack really and there was a Confederate flag hanging over the windows in the front and surrounded by a dozen or so Harleys. Loud music was blaring from inside, and the door was open. The window's glass panes were mostly missing and the rags serving as curtains were blowing in the breeze outside of the house. The yard was either dirt patches or weeds, no grass. Scattered around in the dirt planted cigarette butts looked like a crop, pushed into the soil and growing toward the sky. Crushed beer cans and empty glass liquor bottles littered the yard, along with the smoldering remnants of last nights fire. The make shift fire pit, was surrounded by broken down lawn chairs and tree stumps or car parts that had been used as seating for the prior evening's festivities.

"Home sweet home," he muttered. He veered the poor excuse for a truck into the waist high weeds in front of the shack. He half fell out of the driver's door, holding his broken arm with what remained of his good arm. He couldn't wrap his head around the fact that the man in black had kicked one hand holding a knife, while twisting his other arm as it snapped at the same time. It was as if the fight was happening in slow motion. His chest ached and he had a sharp pain when he inhaled and exhaled, he was sure he also had a couple of broken ribs from the initial kick. His right knee was not right either, as a foot had landed bending it backwards like a pink flamingo. The swollen knee made the jeans pull tight around it, and he thought it was probably broken too. The knee throbbed as he limped into the house. What was worse than the physical pain was the fact that he didn't land a single blow on the other guy. He thought, hell, I've shanked guys in prison before and even killed a man with a brick, how in the hell did this happen to me? At the thought, his anger raged again at Wanda Jane, this is all her fault.

He half walked half-crawled as the flies escorted him in through the open door. The people laying around sleeping off the booze or nodding off from the drugs looked at him with nonchalance. A couple of naked girls, stoned out of their minds, were laying around the room entwined with various naked men. He recognized them as dancers from the 'Lion's Den' strip club he frequented. There laying on the ragged and nasty stained, with substances no one could identify, couch was a skinhead with Nazi Swastikas tattooed on his scalp. It looked like he had been to the same fight Luther had just come from. He fit right in with the riffraff for they were his tribe.

The Swastika man briefly looked at Luther and said, "Shit man, what happened to you? Looks like you met the same guy I did last night."

"Shut the fuck up," Luther sneered back at him. He dragged his aching leg and broken bones to a back room. There a mattress lay on the floor and he flopped onto it, yelping quietly as he went down.

Luther reached under the mattress pulled out a whiskey bottle, and took a long swig straight from the bottle. The liquor burned his busted mouth as he took it in, but it had a pleasant familiar burn going down his gullet. He felt the fireball hit his belly and he paused, and then took another drink, gulping longer this time. Finally, hoisting the bottle and tilting his head backwards, he just opened his throat and let the amber liquid slide down, not even bothering to swallow. He was not savoring the taste of the liquor, he was not just drinking, he was getting drunk, and there was a difference. After repeating the process a few times, the burning in his mouth and gut subsided and replaced by a warm pleasant feeling finally. It felt as if he was riding a wave and floating away, mission accomplished he thought. While the pain was still with him, it diminished registering in what little brain cells he had left. He closed his good eye that wasn't already swollen shut and passed out.

Luther's awoke to someone pulling him up from the mattress and slapping him hard across the face. His arm, ribs, and knee shooting with pain, worse than the painful slap on the face. "What, Get the fuck off me!" He squealed aloud.

Charlie grabbed him by the scruff of the neck and shook him like a ragdoll. "Wake up you bastard," he said.

"Ok, I'm awake, what are you doing man?" Luther asked.

Charlie started screaming into his face, like the Marine he was. "Tell me you piece of shit, why you would attack that girl in the truck stop? What in the fuck is wrong with you? You are and idiot, you know that. You're gonna screw up everything you dickwad." He tossed him back on the stained mattress like a piece of garbage.

"I'm gonna tell you one time only, you are to keep away from that girl. Do you hear me, asshole? Next time, I will cut off your head and piss down your neck, do you understand me?" He stared hard at him.

"Answer me, shit face, do you understand me?" Charlie asked.

"Yeah, yeah I hear you," Luther said looking down at his feet, afraid to look into Charlie's eyes.

"Now, I have to go try to fix this mess, you stupid fucker." Charlie spun on his heels, and while stepping over bodies, stormed out the door.

Unbeknownst to anyone, Eli lay on his belly in the

tall grass on a knoll outside the house. He watched with binoculars at what unfolded through the bedroom window. Eli was puzzled, but he was even more worried about JW by what he just witnessed. He needed a plan of action, just providing a report was no longer acceptable to him. His conscience would not permit him to walk away from this situation and abandon this innocent woman to these evil people.

He slithered out of the grass, back to a nearby road where he had stashed the rental car unnoticed. He would tail Charlie later tonight, as he was sure he was on his way back to the B&B to console JW. Eli would develop a plan to protect JW and take down those intent on harming her.

# TWENTY-FOUR

Charlie stashed his gear in the back seat of his pickup truck. He didn't want JW to know that he had gone to war on her behalf. Fortunately, he didn't need to use the weapons since Luther was a cowardly piece of shit, that only beat on women and kids or anyone that couldn't fight back. From Luther's injury, it looked like somebody had tried to help JW today, and did an exemplary job in working Luther over. He chuckled inwardly at the thought, and I wouldn't mind meeting that guy one-day to see what he could do against me. It might be fun.

Katie ran to see him when he hopped up the steps. "Thank God, I have been worried sick about you."

"I'm fine sis, you know me. How's my girl?" He asked, not stopping or waiting for an answer. He walked straight down the hall to JW's door. He pecked lightly on the door, and tried the knob at the same time and found it open. He entered the dimly lit room and saw JW laying on the bed with an ice pack wrapped in a towel on her face and a damp washcloth over her eyes. He sat down beside her and leaned down to her face, picking up the washcloth and said, "Anybody in there?"

She tried to smile, but her lip hurt and she winced as she said, "I'm afraid I am."

Gently he began to sprinkle baby soft kisses starting at her hairline and trailing around her face, careful not to touch the tender bruises and whelps. He muttered sweet and soft soothing words to her, telling her how beautiful, wonderful, and precious she was to him, and that if anything ever happened to her he didn't know how he could survive this life alone. He then professed his love to her repeatedly. She began to believe him. She patted the bed next to her and without words; he crawled in beside her and spooned her in his strong embrace. They both drifted off to a sweet sleep together, and it seemed as if all was right with the world. She thought as she was floating away, so this is what having someone to rely upon and share life with feels like. I like it, and it feels good. She pushed her deep insecurities and fears away and just for this one moment, she was going to enjoy this feeling. So, she pulled him tighter, spooning against her backside and snuggled into his curves and slept soundly for the first time since she was nine years old.

She awoke when he started to stir beside her, and realized that it was nearing sundown. He said, "Umm, hey beautiful, I could get used to this," as he squeezed her a little. "But I'm hungry, how about we grab some chow?"

After she ate some soup with her sore mouth, she broached a subject with Charlie. "What would you think about going to New York with me for a few days? You could see where I live, and work, and meet Joseph—Leah's husband, and spend some time with me without distraction?"

"How long would you plan for us to be gone?" He asks.

"I was thinking maybe a week, they could do without you around here for that long," she said.

"Let me make a few calls, but it sounds like a great idea." He smiled.

JW was excited and nervous at the same time, what if he didn't fit into her world. She could not give up her life and live here fulltime. This would be a trial run to see if they could mesh their lives together. Could they make something out of the relationship that would work for both of them? She was giddy with anticipation, and they planned to head to New York as soon as they could book a flight.

They landed at LaGuardia the next day, JW was ecstatic to be able to show Charlie her city. A quick Uber ride and they were at her apartment in under 15 minutes after landing. Charlie had been to New York in the past; however, not with his own private tour guide or an apartment with a doorman across from Central Park in Manhattan. This would be a completely new experience, and he was worried about fitting into her world too. She tried to reassure him, that it was a pretty small circle of friends, and most were acquaintances except for the Levy and Wasserman families. Those people were family to her and it was important that they like him, and he like them.

After they got to the apartment, first on the agenda was a walk around the neighborhood to the local grocer for basics like milk, eggs, bread, cheese, peanut butter, and fresh cut flowers. Most of their meals would be in the wonderful restaurants she had found over the years of living here. Of course, one of their evening meals would be required at Leah and Joseph's home, and one evening's meal at Mother Wassermann's. Other than those commitments, they were on their own.

She also planned some typical tourist events for his benefit. She booked the Downtown Loop nighttime bus tour, it was onboard the open-top double-decker sightseeing big red bus. They would see the Times Square North, along 47th St and 7th Avenue. If they timed it right, they could visit the Empire State Building and see the city lights.

She had planned other activities for each day they were in town, and one day she dedicated to Leah and Joseph's gallery to see her art installation exhibit. They would also visit the Museum of Modern Art. As an artist, the MOMA was one of her most favorite venues. She would take him to the 911 Memorial, and the famous charging bull on Wall Street. Evening events planned were to take in some long-running plays on Broadway, and maybe even some off Broadway. Maybe they could even get into the Jimmy Fallon Tonight Show, she had been there done that but would go again if Charlie wanted to go. Of course, they would visit the pizza shops along Times Square and she would teach him how to fold a slice for like a New Yorker. She would also like Charlie to go to a jazz club she liked, she couldn't wait for him to hold her and dance with her slow, and sexy leading her around the dance floor while the music played. Just that thought got her a little excited.

# TWENTY-FIVE

On their first evening in the city, they had dinner at her favorite restaurant, Bobby Flay's Gato. The reservation was in JW's name—so they could get a table at a spur of the moment, and after sitting and enjoying cocktails, Bobby dropped by the table to say hello to JW. Charlie was a little jealous when Bobby warmly kissed JW on the cheek and told her he had missed seeing her in the restaurant lately. She introduced Charlie as an old friend visiting from the South, and Bobby said he would personally prepare their meal, and see them before they left for a review.

They shared an appetizer of oven-roasted shrimp, prepared with diavolo oil and oregano. The flavor was unbelievable, and the shrimp was large and succulent. For a main course, they both ordered the thick rib eye with spice crust and romesco butter. Charlie ordered his rare, and they paired their steaks with a long green beans with harissa Tunisian hot chili pepper paste, and crispy shallots. Bobby did not disappoint, and he joined them for a dessert and coffee, on the house. Bobby regaled Charlie with the story of his purchase of a JW DuValle painting now hanging in his apartment, and how much joy it brought to him each time he walked by and looked at it. Anyone that visits his home remarks on how it fits perfectly in the space. He was clearly a happy customer and an admirer. Charlie beamed with pride.

After dinner, they went to a jazz club for cocktails and cheek to cheek dancing. She was not disappointed with his attention or his dance moves. The way he held her and led her adroitly around the small and dimly lit room as the music infiltrated their senses. She became closer and closer to him and it was the most romantic evening she had enjoyed in a long time. The date ended too soon, but the good news was Charlie went home with her too.

The evening continued at her apartment. Upon entering her door, JW asked Alexa to begin her playlist as she selected the perfect bottle of wine. She chose the cult wine, Cloudburst's Cabernet Sauvignon Red, Opus One 2016, which was a hard to get from the Margaret River region, in the southwest corner of Australian, and retails for over $300 a bottle. Each bottle's grapes are pruned, picked, fermented, and bottled all by hand, including the bottle number. The tiny vineyard only produces 550 cases a year and sells out instantly, it is hard to get which makes it all the more desirable. Charlie produced a handmade cigar, which he acquired from the tobacconist on the street corner. She noticed he preferred the Cohibo Macassar Double Corona, retailing for $31 each. They both had expensive taste, she thought to herself. They sat on her small balcony overlooking Central Park with their individualized vices of cigars and wine to continue their enchanted evening.

She thought it was an appropriate time to take the relationship deeper, since Charlie was professing his love for her relentlessly. She could not utter those words to him yet, but she was on the precipice. She needed to know more about this man before her. She wanted to understand his dreams and desires in life. She needed to know they would be able to chase them together while enduring the day-to-day monotony of life. She wanted to experience the moments to remember in the days you forget.

She poured the wine and sipped to taste. Once the warm deep blackcurrant colored liquid entered her mouth, she began to feel its effects, from her nose to her toes. It was soft and spicy, tasted of violet, blackcurrant, raspberry, and dark plum, with a chocolaty mocha hint.

"Mm mm, this is really good," she said. "Try this Charlie," as she handed him a long-stemmed glass, and then she observed him closely. Would he gulp it or savor it, she wondered?

He swirled the wine around in the glass, he held by the stem, so as not to heat the wine with his hand. Swirling just enough to aerate the liquid, and release the aromas before he took his first delicate sip. The swirling released the tiny compounds that floated on evaporating alcohol, which he breathed deeply, as a large part of wine enjoyment is in the ability to smell the flavor.

She smiled as he savored every moment, from anticipation, presentation, smell, and finally consumption. The metaphor was obvious, this is how he makes love, she thought. Taking his time and savoring each moment, and she became aroused at the thought.

At that particular moment, the playlist started to

play and Michael Bolton began to sing out "When a Man Loves a Woman." Charlie groaned and sat the wine glass down and pulled her close to his taut chest, took her hand in his, folded his arm between her and him and started swaying, leading her to the music. The sexual tension was so intense that it was all she could do to keep from dancing him toward her bedroom. Nevertheless, she was not going to go there until she was sure. There was still a very difficult conversation to have with this man, before she would be ready.

After their dance, they pulled away hesitantly from each other's bodies and went back to the deck trying to pretend what just happened hadn't. It was hard to speak for a few minutes, but then they picked up where they left off. At some point in the evening, Charlie began to open up to her about his active duty days. He told her that it took many years for him to try to get his head screwed back on straight after being in Afghanistan.

He said, "You know the Marine's call us jarheads for a reason. They take a young starry-eyed kid, unscrew his head, fill it with shit, and then screw the lid back on—hence jarheads." She just let him talk until he was done; she realized that's what he needed at this moment.

He surprised her when said whispered softly while rubbing her thumb between his fingers, 'I am a forest, and a night of dark trees: but he, who is not afraid of my darkness, will find banks full of roses under my cypresses.' "That's Nietzsche, one of my favorites."

Charlie did everything right tonight, and she felt herself falling for him, and this was only their first night together in the Big Apple.

# TWENTY-SIX

The amazing week in New York with Charlie was ending and it had been all she had hoped it would be. Charlie flourished in the city that never sleeps, he was fun, and up for anything that she suggested. He was the perfect companion, and fit right in with her lifestyle. He even surprised her with his depth of knowledge of the arts, his love of the culture and the ease he assimilated to her world.

He had one more test tonight, they had dinner planned at Leah and Joseph Levy's apartment, and Mother Wasserman would be joining them. JW was nervous for her pseudo family to meet her possible future family. Then she and Charlie planned to be head back to Kentucky together. There was one last piece of business JW wanted to take care of at the farm, and she wanted Charlie to be there with her when she did.

Arriving late for dinner, as usual, she rang the Levy's doorbell. Leah welcomed her guest into their home and JW was surprised to see Eli sitting on the living room sofa. This was the first time she had seen him, since he had saved her from Luther's attack at the truck stop. She hoped that he did not mention that day to Charlie, as she didn't want him to know anything about Eli or his investigation. She was sure that if Charlie found out she was looking into his background that he would be devastated and angry enough to end the relationship. She was disappointed and ashamed of herself for even having Joseph hire his cousin to snoop on Charlie. She would be anxious all night, as long as Eli was in the room.

Joseph introduced Eli as his cousin visiting from Israel and it was uneventful, no questions asked. The dinner Leah prepared was sumptuous and the conversation flowed freely. Mother Wasserman was delighted to be included in JW's new romance and she did her best to convince Charlie that JW was the catch and he better not let her get away. If Mother Wasserman only knew who was dragging their feet, she would laugh. Charlie was charming, and saying all the right things. JW did notice that Joseph and Eli seemed uneasy and they spoke in clipped sentences, several times, she saw their heads close together, and whispers between them. Was she being paranoid again? She would have to question Leah tomorrow to find out what was going on between the two of them. The evening was over too soon, they said their goodnights and the couple decided to walk leisurely home and enjoy their last night in the city.

As dumb luck would have it, about a block from their apartment a hopped up dope sick punk decided this couple looked like easy victims tonight. Evidently, this dude was not in his right mind, when he pulled out the gun Charlie's 'Spidey Sense' kicked in. Charlie quickly stepped between JW and the gunman to shield her. He said very calmly, "OK, I'm going to reach in my jacket and pull out my wallet real slow, don't get itchy on me, K."

In a motion so fast that she could hardly keep up

with his movements, Charlie grabbed and twisted his gun hand until she heard the wrist cleanly snap. He then used his elbow on the man's face and nose, turned quickly, and smoothly put a knee to his groin and it was over. She watched the gunman melt into the ground, like the wicked witch of the west in the rain. Charlie didn't even break a sweat, and he completely disabled the man in a matter of seconds. The movements reminded her of the attack in the truck stop and Eli's prompt dispatch of Luther. She was in awe of their abilities, who taught these men to fight like this, she wondered.

After things calmed down, the police did their jobs, and they were back safely in her apartment Charlie said, "I need a shower to wash the scumbag off me, will you excuse me for a minute?"

"Of course, take your time."

It was a quick shower and he came out the bathroom door wrapped in a towel from the waist down. Uh oh, this does not bode well for me she thought, as her eyes scanned the muscular man that stood before her drying his close-cropped hair with a spare towel. He still wore dog tags around his neck, and she could see every ripple in the six-pack on his abdomen. He had a tattoo on one bicep, it looked like a Marine logo of some type, but she had trouble concentrating on the tatt with all the other distractions.

He walked closer to her as he held out his arms and flicked his fingers with a come to me motion. She did as he asked. She was powerless, and couldn't help herself.

The next thing she noticed was his smell, it was fresh with just a hint of aftershave, nothing overpowering. She always found Charlie subtle in all ways. Next, she felt the substantial bulge under the towel pressing firmly against her body. He wanted her to feel him hard, as it was his way of asking without saying a word.

She was taking in his whole body with all of her senses, and then she noticed on his left breast, over his heart, there was a light scar—an SS. Seared into his skin, it was a brand. She let her fingers roam over it and her mind questioned who would do this? She knew she needed to change the subject, and get both their minds off what was beneath that towel.

"Tell me about this," as she tapped the scar.

Instead, he said, "You know you make me crazy, I want you so bad."

"I want you too Charlie, but not yet, not tonight. I have to tell you something and it may change your mind about me. We need to talk first." Charlie shook his head as if he understood and moaned and went to put his pants on.

She was sitting on the sofa when he got back and she was softly crying. This was one of the most difficult conversations of her life, and she was so scared. She had never told anyone this story before, this was a secret that she had planned to take with her to her grave. He deserved to know, as this would affect anyone that wanted a sexual relationship with her, and he had a right to know.

She began as her lip trembled, "I'm going to tell you a story, it's not a pretty story, but please don't say anything until I'm done. This is so hard for me."

JW proceeded to tell of the summer she was nine, her mother was sick and in the hospital for a week and daddy was working. Like so many other weeks, she went to go stay with Aunt Minnie. The farm was usually fun for her, and she loved playing with all the animals. There were cats, dogs, chickens, goats, and an old pair of horses that used to work the fields, and a pond where she would swim. She loved it, until this visit. This was when her nightmares began.

"One night as I was curled sleeping soundly in the side bedroom under an old quilt, someone opened the window and climbed into the room. I felt a presence and opened my eyes so innocently, and there he was on top of me—Luther.

He was seven years older—sixteen, and I was still a baby. He put his hand over my mouth and threatened to kill me like he did those kittens in the barn, when I was six. I was so afraid, and he was so cruel. He crawled into my bed and raped me the first time, when I was nine years old. It hurt so bad, there was so much blood. The nightmare continued nightly the week I was there, and he proceeded to do other things to me, which I'll leave to the imagination. Things no little girl should ever be subjected. The damage was more than physical. He damaged me for any man. Charlie, I still have nightmares, I can't be intimate with anyone, and I never have. I suffer flashbacks, freeze, have anxiety attacks, and run away. I am ruined and I am damaged goods. So if you don't want me, I understand." She sobbed and put her head in her hands in her lap.

Charlie kneeled before her, and cradled her and began soothing her, "Oh baby, I'm so sorry, it's ok, please don't cry. I got you, I got you. You are NOT damaged," he said forcefully. "I wanted to kill that piece of shit for what he did to you at the diner, I definitely want to finish him now," he spit out the words with hatred. "Babe, we will work on this together, it'll be ok."

She raised her head, and said, "You don't hate me, I'm so ashamed."

"JW, my God, you were a little girl, you were a victim—you should never be ashamed of this, but you sure as hell should be mad. Let's go home baby, I got you." Charlie rocked her like the nine-year-old girl she was inside at this moment. For once since that fateful week, she began to have hope that maybe she could find healing, and love.

# TWENTY-SEVEN

She hated to see Charlie go, but JW needed some serious studio time to process her feelings. Her best work always happened when she was high or low in her emotional state. She was high, after the week she had played in her backyard with Charlie. He was too good to be true, wasn't he, she asked herself smiling?

Charlie hated to leave her just as much, but his trucking firm and the farming needed his attention. The summer was drawing to a close, which meant the harvest would soon begin, and after that, the autumn rains moved into the South. Farming had changed tremendously since his dad began farming the 300-acre homestead in the '70's. To become a farmer today, you needed a lot of good credit, equipment, land, farmhands and a head for economics. All of this cost money, and was at the mercy of the weather. Harvest season was always a major undertaking for the now over 3000-acres of farmland Charlie planted in corn and soybean. The original family farm was 300 acres, which abutted JW's inheritance. However, Charlie with high aspirations had expanded his operations, across the county. Today he leased or owned the 2700 acres of additional farmland that he planted in corn and soybeans, and was always in the market for more land.

He usually drove one of his 16 row shiny new

International Harvester combines, but also hired a driver for the second. These behemoths of the fields cost over $500K each. He had also purchased grain carts for collection at the ends of the mile long rows to enhance productivity. No matter how many rows you picked or how fast you ran the combine, if you could not dump it into a grain truck, and haul it to a bin or grain elevator, you were wasting time sitting on a full and expensive piece of farm equipment idling in the field. He also hired and scheduled grain trucks for collection to haul the load to the grain elevators. The cash outlay wasn't just for harvest, he also had invested in planters, and sprayers for planting the crops, add to that cost the seed, fertilizer, maintenance and labor. It was a cash intensive operation and he had financed it to the hilt.

Selling the grain was also another major economic decision. He employed software programs that helped determine cost of production, yield per acre, and calculating break-even price. On top of that, he also had to make sure he sold the crops at a price that covered cost and made a profit, which meant developing a diversification and hedging plan, and he always bought crop insurance, of course. Part of his hedging plan, was lessening the risk of loss in the cash market by taking an opposite position in the futures market.

This was no longer his daddy's small farming operation. Cooper Farming LLC was a business that ran on massive lines of credit, loans, futures, options, and other financial paper, it was complex, and one misstep was all it would take to spell disaster. The actual harvest was like a dance in the field, everyone had their position, and the timing had to be precise. His goal was to hit the sweet spot of harvest, perfect crop, perfect weather, perfect machinery, and perfect market. Charlie could control the crop for the most part, the machinery, and hedge his bet, but he was always at the mercy of the weather. And so, it was and will always be that the weather is the bane of the farmer, no matter the size of the operation.

He ran two large combines with the latest and greatest electronic controls and his loop dump and transport plan estimated a 20-day harvest plan, based on sunup to sundown operation. He usually ran 8 a.m. to midnight, when weather was perfect and could cut that time down to a 10-day harvest. Driver fatigue and equipment breakage, or any hiccup in the transport would lengthen that plan and eat into profits, if any. Farming was not the faint of heart or uneducated.

It took a great deal of logistics, but he was good at moving things. He smiled to himself as he thought about all the things that he moved around, people would be shocked if they only knew. Hell, he thought, sometimes I shock myself at what I do.

JW also had work to do of her own. She had not been in the studio since her last gallery show. She had needed the break since she had not had a vacation, ever. Her bank account was flush from the sold-out show Leah and Joseph had pulled off again and her print business did very well and guaranteed a steady source of income. She was walking on clouds from the week with Charlie and she wanted to express that on a canvas. She wanted to paint love, hope, and happiness, and intended to spend the next three weeks doing just that in the studio. She would then take a trip to see Charlie, while the paint dried. If everything went according to plan, the canvas would be ready for varnish when she returned.

During her time at the B&B, she had been taking photos and sketching the scenery in her inspiration book. The pages were brimming with the sultry summer colors and vivid blooms of the south, and compositions that evoked feelings deep down into her soul. Although portraiture was not her specialty, she couldn't help but draw Charlie's exquisite form. He was beautiful to look at and she was contemplating how to incorporate him into a series she was thinking about, she was smitten with him.

Today was to be a studio day and she put on her painting clothes and walked the few blocks to the back door of the gallery to face the daunting white canvas. The most difficult an intimidating thing for an artist is to make the first brushstroke on the white. To get herself in the mood, she would start her music and had a playlist that would try to evoke what she was feeling. Each canvas also resonated its own feeling, as soon as she sat down on the chair and picked up a brush, it would tell her what it wanted to be. The goal would be to match all three things together and see it in her mind. Her music would start, she would brew her a tea or coffee, and select a pencil or charcoal that she would run her fingers over. The graphite would tell her fingers where to lay down the first mark, her mind had a finished picture in her head before the first line was drawn, and the sketch in the book kept her on track. Her sketches or photographs helped her to remember the lights and darks, where the sunlight was in the sky that day. Her notes told her what the air smelled like, the humidity of the air and the shape of the clouds overhead. The feelings of the surrounding were as important as the colors she blended on the palette. She was successful in abstract and in realism, lately her paintings were the later.

She would make the initial faint sketches in graphite, working from light to dark, and the backgrounds going down first. The palette held her pre-determined base colors, that she would magically mix into the right tones and values that harmonized where needed, this part came so naturally to her. She thoughtfully placed her strokes, to guide the viewer's eye around the canvas. At this stage of the creative process, the painting always looked bad, and they always look bad before they looked good. Funny how that worked, she thought, but it was the same every time. She always had to fight the urge to trash the work at the early stage, then like a caterpillar, it would morph into a beautiful butterfly—suddenly appearing in the mesh of colors. Her mind's eye would see it emerge, and when the magic happened, she was primed and ready to go. She ran with the mystical unveiling appearing before her, she knew where to lay the paint on or scrape it off, where to add linseed oil or rub it off, and when to use the palette knife. Then she would finally apply the accents and fine brushwork needed that set her apart in the art world. This process would take sweet time, she didn't rush it, she let it speak to her. Some days she could only give a few hours and would need to take time out to regroup, stop, and do something else while her mind worked out the problem with the canvas. Other times the daylight ran into nighttime and she was lost in a time and space, she was unaware to the time or hunger and she couldn't stop painting.

After years of following this process and allowing it to emerge, she realized this is what made her an artist. Her art is just as her life, fighting every urge to give up and quit when it becomes unbearable. She feels the birthing pangs physically, and with her whole being. Savoring and honoring them instead of dismissing them, it is knowing that she is pushing something new into the world, something fresh, clean, and untarnished.

She would use her inner strength to push, pull, and then fan the small spark to keep it smoldering, until the air caught it and ignited the canvas with the fire. This is how she created her art.

# TWENTY-EIGHT

It had been three weeks since she had seen Charlie, they had talked on the telephone several times a day, but she longed to touch him and to smell his essence. She had taken the quick flight from New York back to Kentucky, and was already in the rental car, still thinking about Charlie. She had a very productive time in the studio though, and the piece she had birthed was nearing completion. She had yet to show it to Leah, because she was still very protective of it, but she was close to the unveiling. It was in the drying process, she would spend some time with Charlie, and then when she got back to the studio she would put the finish on the canvas.

She sped along I65 South erasing the miles between her and Charlie, hoping she would not get a speeding ticket, and she made it to the B&B in record time. It was still a very hot and humid August day in Kentucky, and when she opened the car door the air hit her like a slap in the face it was so heavy. Tiny no-see-ums jumped onto her skin as she walked the flower lined stone path up to the porch. She clawed at the invisible bites and smacked at sweat bees that would not leave her alone. Perspiration broke out all over her body just from lifting her bags from the car, so her first stop would be a cool shower. Katie had her room ready, as usual, and a snack for her after the laborious trip. Coming to the farm was like coming home, and she couldn't wait to see Charlie again.

She didn't have to wait long; she was just out of the shower in a terry cloth robe with her hair wrapped in a towel when she heard him knock at the door. Hey handsome she said as she opened the door, and there he stood, looking better than she remembered. Time does make the heart grow fonder she thought. He quickly took her in his arms and walked her backwards shutting the door with his foot behind him, as he was kissing her hard and sloppy, full on the mouth. Showing her with his body how excited, he was to see her. When her knees felt the bed behind her, she lay down and he found the perfect landing spot right beside her. She was still in his embrace, with his mouth eagerly tasting her and she did not resist him. His hands began to search for her beneath the robe, starting with her breast. When he felt her erect nipples, he gently pinched and twisted them between his fingers. It reflexively elicited her back and neck to arch and she couldn't stifle the moan, which stirred him on even more. He moved his mouth from her mouth to her nipple and began sucking and biting gently and painfully with his teeth, alternating between each of them. It hurt just right. She shuddered, as she jerked his t-shirt over his head and began clawing his naked back and wrapping her legs around his chest. He then lifted her fully onto the bed and spreads open her robe to see all of her splendid naked body. Her legs were amazingly long and ended at just the right spot, he thought. She did not care what he did, and her mind was already where he wished his body were. He looked hungrily at her mound of pubic hair and touched her tenuously between her legs to see if she would let him continue. She did, he used his finger and gently touched her soft fleshy wetness. He was shaking with anticipation of what was to come….then the flashback came on her like a bucket of ice-cold water.

She screamed loudly, "NO, NO, NO, please stop," as she scrambled away. "I can't," as she jumped up, and pulling the robe around her she went running to the bathroom and locked the door.

Charlie gave out a loud moan, as he rolled over, saying, and "You have got to be kidding me." He heard the shower running again, and for a long time, he lay there calming himself down. When she did not come out after a while, he left the room, angrily shutting the door behind him. This chick has some serious issues, he thought to himself. I don't know if she's worth all this shit. He got into his truck and spun gravel and he sped away, to find relief somewhere else tonight.

After the incident JW, felt full of feelings, they were across the board. She was sad, guilty, ashamed, sorry, and embarrassed. She wasn't sure which one was the right one, or if there was a 'right' one. She hoped Charlie could forgive her, and she hoped that one day she would be able to be with him in the way they both wanted. She wasn't sure how to overcome the debilitating memories that kept hijacking her mind. She tried her best to exorcise them from her brain, to no avail. She had years of counseling, cognitive behavior therapy, regression therapy and pharmaceutical therapy. Nothing seemed to work, maybe it never would, and she could not forgive the animal that had stolen this part of her life from her.

It suddenly dawned on her that she was being a victim still. Until she became a survivor, she would never be free from the damage Luther had done. But, how would she do that? She would have to think long and hard and try to find the answer, and until she did, she thought she was no good to anyone. So tonight would be an early to bed night and one of tossing and turning with a slideshow of horrors from her childhood.

Charlie on the other hand, pulled into the Sugar Shack and bought a cold six-pack, and let his truck take him to a small brick house on the outskirts of town. The big yellow school bus was parked in the lean-to covering it beside the drive. Charlie pulled his pickup truck around behind the building to hide it from view of the road, and he had called on his way over so she could palm the kids off on her mother for the night. Brenda Johnson was standing in the kitchen doorway when he walked up the back steps. She pulled him close and said, "I've sure missed you, what's kept you so long honey?"

Just like that, Charlie cheated on JW, before he had ever been faithful the first time. This was a weekly event. Theirs had been an ongoing affair since returning from the Marines, interrupted only when one or both of them had taken a new temporary lover. No matter how hard he tried, he kept coming back around to the old flame like the moth to the fire, and she too.

Even though he hated cheating, it had become the new norm for Charlie. He even justified his actions because JW couldn't bring herself to be with a real man. He had tried all his tricks to warm her up, but she was a frigid, ice queen, he thought. She was broken, and he didn't like broken people. He didn't want to deal with their issues, nor take the time needed to try to fix them. Not his problem he thought and he needed sex. She tortured him with her teasing and then turning him away. He was tired of playing her games. He thought, some men would have kept going, not stopping until they got what they wanted. He gave himself credit for that.

Brenda had drinks poured and scented candles burning in the bedroom, she knew what Charlie had come for and she was eager to provide it. The days of her getting any boy she wanted in high school were well behind her, so she took love where she could find it. Charlie was the only one that wanted her now days, and even that was a well-kept secret. Only her ex-husband knew about Charlie. The ex-had enough, finally leaving after catching her not just once, but more than twice with her unattainable lover boy. The only problem she had with the current arrangement was that Charlie had introduced JW into their love triangle. She didn't like it, and wasn't going to give Charlie up without a fight. She had been working behind the scenes to drive JW out of town since she had arrived, which hadn't worked yet. But, she just needed to turn up the heat a notch hotter and be rid of her once and for all. Charlie would get over it eventually and it would be back to their business as usual arrangement.

Charlie started drinking before he got out of the truck and he needed liquid encouragement for a night with Brenda. He did have a conscience after all, he believed that had been dead and buried after Afghanistan, but guessed not. In the bedroom, he had a few more shots to numb his brain, then he could do the deed and imagine it was JW—not Brenda under him. When he was done, he rolled over and went to sleep for a few hours. As usual, when he woke up in the middle of the night, he would slip out of the house in secret and no one would suspect a thing.

Except tonight camouflaged and laying in a ditch behind the house, was an Israeli Mossad agent, Eli. Who had filmed the entry and exit from the house and logged it in his little black notebook with the other damaging information about the doings of the unfaithful Charlie. Eli was saddened at the thought of having to tell of this infidelity to JW, who had enchanted him at first glance. He mourned her loss of love, and blasphemed Charlie for damaging the trust and adoration she had bestowed upon him. Oh, how he longed to be that man blessed with the treasure of JW, the love she exuded from her eyes when she looked at him. He would never have forsaken her as Charlie had.

# TWENTY-NINE

The following morning, JW started calling Charlie around 8 a.m. She had to apologize and tell him she had been thinking about how to exorcise the demon from her mind. She was excited for what she had dreamt up and knew he would be all in for the adventure. He didn't answer her calls until the third try around 10 a.m.; she knew he was sending a message that he was still angry with her. She began apologizing for her actions the night before, she was so ashamed, and she promised him it would never happen again. After a few minutes, he warmed up to her and she told him her plan, the timing and weather were perfect to carry out the scheme. There had been a light rain falling all night and all day, so the ground was wet and muddy, which lessened the risk of a wildfire. She asked Charlie to buy her a 5-gallon can of gasoline, and to pick her up at sundown tonight. As she expected, he was all in, she told him to dress in all black so they would not stand out in the darkness and she would be ready when he got there.

Promptly at dusk, Charlie arrived at the B&B. JW looked like a cat burglar in her tight gear. She had on tight black leggings, black Doc Martin boots, with a black nylon long sleeve shirt and she had pinned up her long hair, and stuffed it under a black ball cap. She was ready to go undercover. The gasoline was in a red plastic can with a black funnel sat in the bed of the pickup truck. She had bought a disposable butane lighter from the Dollar General Store earlier that day, when she had gone shopping for her black cat burglar clothing. She was now ready to cremate the ghostly remains of her childhood.

They drove without small talk, and she noticed Charlie had some scratch marks on his arms, which she attributed to working on the farm today. They pulled up the hill drive to the front of Aunt Minnie's house and barn. She said, "Let's do this."

He didn't take persuasion, she hopped out of the big truck, and Charlie retrieved the gas can and carried it to the barn for her. She took it from him, and spread half the can around the base of the barn, and then she headed toward the house. She did the same thing around the rundown dark house and she was almost giddy with excitement. As she doused the wooden frame, she curse Luther and what had happened here so many nightmares ago. After the can had given up its last drop, she threw it into the house and said, "Stand back."

She clicked the butane lighter one time, until the flame sparked to life. With an exhale, she touched the flame to the wet gas trail and it swooshed to ignite. She was exhilarated and ran towards the barn, as she wanted them both to go up in flames together. When the blaze grew and flames shot licking into the night sky, she smiled and she watched the buildings and felt the heat from the inferno.

She whispered through clenched teeth, "burn baby, burn."

They stayed at the farm and tended the flame for

hours so that it would not escape and create a wildfire. The light rain that fell made this job easy. When the house and barn had finally collapsed and smoldered, they stirred the last of the fires with a shovel from Charlie's truck and watched the raindrops extinguish the rest. It was a relief to JW, she felt as if she had cremated a demon tonight, and her mind immediately switched from victim to victor mode. She was finally on her way to healing from the abuse. Now all she needed to do was deal with Luther and she would be finally free.

She could also focus on Charlie and healing their relationship, if it wasn't too late for them. She saw life with Charlie as a real possibility and she knew they could easily integrate into each other's world, if he still wanted her. He was acting very strangely tonight. She couldn't quite understand why, she thought they had overcome the incident from last night. Maybe they had not. She wanted to talk it out with him, but not here, this place still felt like it carried bad juju. She needed a place of healing and peace to rectify their relationship.

"Charlie, we need to go someplace to talk about what happened last night, any ideas?" She said.

"Yeah, let me take you to a place I like to go think sometimes, you up for it?" He asked.

She nodded yes, and they piled in the truck and he drove away. She felt oddly at peace and proud of herself at the same time, over the burned house and barn, and she glanced in the trucks side mirror. She saw the house's outline laying on the ground, still smoldering like a roaring dragon that she had slain.

She smiled slyly as she also thought how pissed Luther would be when he found out what she had done. She secretly hoped he came for her one more time, she had something to prove and hoped she could stand up to him. The truck rattled along the road, and Charlie reached for her hand. Maybe there is hope for us after all, she thought.

He drove into the night and she had no idea where they were going, but being with Charlie holding her hand was all that mattered to her. He pulled off the main road onto a gravel lane and the roadway trailed upwards, ruts were deep in the so-called road, but Charlie engaged the 4-wheel drive and the truck lurched forward through the brush scraping the sides of the vehicle. The deeper into the woods and higher the incline, the more JW fought with her anxiety.

"Charlie, where are we going, I'm getting a little nervous," her voice tremored.

"Don't worry, my love, it'll be worth it." He said.

The truck kept climbing and scraping, Charlie looked like he knew what he was doing, and that helped to settle her nerves. She trusted him completely, and then she wondered should I be so trusting? No one on earth knows where I am right now, but Charlie. She was just getting ready to tell him to take her back, when he pulled to a stop.

"We're here," he said.

He got out of the truck into the tall weeds, fought through them to get to her side, and opened her door, asking for her hand. He also, pulled a long black flashlight from the back floorboard and turned it on, lighting a path. He held her closely, so that she would not fall in the wet, slick grass, as they approached a large boulder.

"Get behind me and put your hands on my waist, follow behind me, and be careful," he ordered more that ask.

She did what he said, but she was starting to get very anxious, and her gut was telling her to turn back. Then he stopped, and said, "We're here, sit down beside me, I want to show you something." She did as he said, and there below was the entire world to see. The starlights twinkled above them, and the town and homes below them, and the full moon shone on the valley and waters beneath them. It was indescribable, and she was in awe of the beauty of the earth that night.

"Charlie, this is so beautiful, how did you ever find this spot?" She asked.

"This is actually a well-known place around these parts, this is called Pilot's Rock," he said. Then he went on to explain that his uncle used to bring him hunting in these woods, and that the rock was a popular hangout when he was in high school. Kids used to bring their girls up here, and their Boones Farm or Dekuyper Sour Apple Pucker and maybe a couple of joints and watch the stars and the moon from this rock. The heat from the sunshine of the day is absorbed into the rock, and gives off its warmth in the evening mist.

He said, "Up here, you didn't have to worry about cops, or anybody disturbing your make out sessions. I've had a lot of good times on this rock," he smiled at her.

"You didn't happen to bring any of those things you mentioned with you, did you?" She asked.

"Well, well let me see," he said, "Just maybe I did," as he pulled out a joint and a brown paper sack with a bottle of Sour Apple Pucker from inside his jacket.

"I certainly, like the way you plan, Mr. Cooper," she said laughing and reaching for the joint. "I haven't done this since I was at Tisch."

And they smoked, and drank and laid on the warm rock looking at the stars and talking until the early morning, watching the sunrise over the sleepy town together. It was one of the best nights of her life.

# THIRTY

When JW and Charlie pulled into the B&B they saw the flashing lights and multitude of cars surrounding the house. They immediately started trying to hide any evidence of their activities from the night before.

"Oh shit," Charlie said, "Do you have any gum or mints?"

"Nope," she couldn't stifle her giggle. "I'm really hungry too."

The Sheriff was standing on the porch and Charlie knew him and called him by name.

"Hey John, what brings y'all out here?" Charlie said nervously.

"I hate to be the bearer of bad news," and he turned to JW and said, "I assume you are Wanda Jane Walker?"

"Yes," she said.

"I need to inform you that your Aunt's house and barn burned to the ground last night," the sheriff said. She tried to remain cool and innocent.

"We also believe the fire to be a case of arson. Of course, if there is no insurance claim filed, there is no illegality with that, but there is something else that is a problem." He said.

Charlie was tense, and JW was trying her best not to give herself away. The sheriff kept talking.

"Where were you last evening?" He asked.

She said, "I was on a date with Charlie here."

"We also need to inform you that in the rubble we found the badly burned remains of a body."

She jerked and looked at Charlie, her eyes wide with horror. "What, you found what, who?" She asked.

"We don't know who the victim was or what they were doing in the house. They could well have been the arsonist and got caught up in their own fire." His voice trailed off then picked up again, "But, we do have a forensic pathologist from the State crime lab looking at the body, and we have a fire inspector gathering evidence from the scene."

JW went white and became upset at the thought of her burning a person alive in that house last night. She looked at Charlie and grabbed his arm.

"In the meantime, you are not to step foot onto that farm. It is an active crime scene, and we advise you that you are to remain available should we need to talk to you again. Is that understood?"

She could barely speak as she squeaked out, "OK." She walked to her room, took off her clothes, and showered the smoke and pot smells off her body. She also tried to wash the guilt away, but that was not as easy to do.

Later that day after Charlie had left to go to the trucking company and Katie had gone to the grocery store, she took the black clothing and boots out behind the house into a bare spot in the field. She had the butane lighter she had used to torch the house, and she flicked it until it ignited. She put the shirt, hat and pants down first, then laid the boots on top of the pile. She ignited the fabric, and it caught quickly. Must have had some of the gas splashed on the clothing she thought. She watched the pile burn, and then she threw the lighter on top of the flames. The boots did not burn. They were just scorched. She then dug a hole with her hand as best she could underneath the ashes, and tried to bury the boots and the remnant metal of the lighter. This will have to do, she thought. She went back into the house and washed her hands, but they never felt clean no matter how much she scrubbed.

Earlier Charlie had left to go to the trucking company to checkup on some business and told her he'd be back later in the day. When he arrived at the trucking parking lot, he pulled up his contact list and punched a familiar number. The person on the other end was an old school chum that just so happened to work for the Sheriff's department, and owed him a big favor.

"Hey buddy, this is Charlie Cooper, I need a payback for that favor I did for you." He proceeded to question him about the charred body they found in the farmhouse.

He heard the friend typing to opened the computer file and the he began to read quietly. "An unidentified male body had been found in the 'puglistic' stance in what was the side bedroom. The body is undergoing an autopsy, have ordered x-rays and a scan, fluids going for toxicology screen. They pulled DNA from subject's internal organs, and running against COVIS. They expect this should be a pretty quick ID and turn-around."

"Can I get you to give me a call when anything comes in, I really need to help a friend out," Charlie got an agreement, and signed off.

Now what to do, he wondered? He realized the first thing he needed to do was to get rid of any evidence linking him to JW's crime. He needed to get rid of his smoky clothes and shoes, so into the building he went. He had a mini-apartment for times he needed to be on 24-seven, and he kept extra clothes there. After a quick shower, he bagged his dirty clothes, boots, and knife and stowed it in a cardboard box. He stuffed other trash on top of it and drove to the county dump. They will never look here or find this in the midst of the whole county's trash, he thought. He made the deposit unnoticed by the landfill operator. Every couple of days, the operator would use a bulldozer to push the trash into a large hole in the ground and cover it over with dirt.

The dump was a streamlined and had only one operator, who was busy at the recycle bins when Charlie drove up. All Charlie had to do was pitch the trash over a small concrete wall into the day's pile of rubbish, and drive away. Charlie smiled proudly at himself, as he started the truck and headed back to the B&B.

As he pulled away, the Israeli shadow was following him undetected, just as he had been since JW's return to town. After Charlie made his deposit at the dump, Eli waited until landfill operator had left for the day, then he quietly climbed the gate and retrieved the box of evidence. This might come in handy someday, he thought, and it wouldn't hurt to have some more insurance. He stashed the box in the trunk of his car and headed back to the B&B to get his eyes on Charlie and to cover JW's back. She didn't realize how much danger she was in and he felt needed to protect her.

# THIRTY-ONE

Charlie returned to the B&B and found Katie in the kitchen prepping dinner. "I need a favor," he said picking up a celery stick and chomping it loudly. "I need an alibi for last night; I was here all night, with you. We had dinner, and then I went to bed early around nine. Got that?"

"Sure Charlie," she looked quizzically at him. "JW?"

"No, I don't know where she was and I don't know what time she left, or when she got back. Got that?" Charlie said sternly.

"Yes sir," Katie saluted when she said it. She could tell by his eyes, he didn't think that was funny.

Katie said, "She's back in her room," and she nodded her head down the hallway toward JW's room. He didn't say a word, just turned around and walked back out the door and left. Katie shrugged her shoulders and went back to chopping vegetables.

JW was in her room, crying, since she had come back from burying her boots in the backfield. She needed to call Leah, she needed her friend, but she was too upset. She couldn't talk without crying. She wailed at the thought of getting Charlie into this mess. All because of her, this was all her fault and she burst into tears again at that thought. She longed for him to hold her, comfort her, and tell her everything would be OK. Where was he? She had tried his cell multiple times, but he would not answer her calls. Did he blame her for the death of the person burned in the fire? She had to convince him that she knew nothing about the body, but she realized it looked bad for her.

She was at one of the lowest points in her life, and she couldn't imaging a way out of this situation. She had torched that house and barn, it was all her doing, and somebody had died. She killed someone in that fire, even if she didn't mean to, it was second-degree murder, she moaned again. She could end up in prison. It would all be over, her life, her career and all that she had worked for would be gone. She might have even lost the only man that ever professed to love her. She was also angry with herself for having believed she could ever find love. She groaned at the foolish thought that Charlie might stick around. No one ever had, she had been on her own since she had memories. She had foolishly, envisioned marriage, and a real family one-day—maybe even kids. She chuckled at once having those ridiculous thoughts. These were things she had only dared hope for in her dreams, and they had been at her fingertips. Now the dreams were gone, just like that, reduced to ashes of a fire. Oh the fire, she thought again. What did I do?

He had almost convinced her that she had worth, but now look at her. She had always believed she was damaged goods and no man would ever want her, then she had met Charlie. With one stupid action, she had possibly destroyed three lives last night, the burn victim, hers, and Charlie's. She couldn't blame him, if he was done with her for good.

She whispered a prayer, "Oh God, what have I done. Please send somebody to help me."

What she didn't know was that God had answered her prayer before she had even known to pray it. Eli was outside already watching, helping, and protecting her. He was perched in a tree line with a clear view of the highway leading into the B&B and both the front and rear entrances to the farmhouse. He had been constantly standing vigil over her, all night in the rain, never leaving his post. He had gathered what he needed about Charlie, but now JW needed him, and he would remain with her. Eli believed her to be in real danger.

Eli felt a spiritual connection to the beautiful soul, and brave woman, and he longed for her to return his feelings. He shook his head as a foolish thought as she barely knew he existed. What he would give to be in Charlie's shoes for she deserved better than what Charlie Cooper would give to her. Eli vowed right there to God, that he would move mountains for her if needed, and he asked God to intervene to help him help her. Eli was a man of faith, and justice, he believed that he and JW were not that different, she just did not know it yet. She needed faith, he thought, and soon she would realize what that meant, in addition to love. He believed one needed to have faith, and true love would find you. Your bashert will always find you, for it is God's way.

Later in the night as Eli was performing his sentry duties, and lightly dozing, he heard a car slowly approach on the main road. It was 3 a.m. as he glanced at his watch. The car's headlights switched off and evading the video cameras, the driver stopped well short of the parking area. They had familiarity with the surroundings and security system. The moonlight shone brightly, and Eli had his recording device ready. When the driver opened the car door, the interior light made a clear identification possible and they crept closer to the house. The culprit quietly placed a note under the windshield wiper of JW's car before returning to their car. Eli continued recording as they backed slowly out of the drive onto road and sped away. Makes sense, he thought, as things were becoming clearer to him with every chess move. He made another note in his little black book of this encounter and remained well hidden in the trees.

The following morning JW made herself get out of bed, showered, and dressed. It was time to take charge of the situation and she decided to start with Charlie. She made with a long overdue call to Leah, to fill her in on the fire, the body, the trouble she brought on her and Charlie. Leah was supportive as always, and told her not to talk to anyone—about anything. She also suggested quickly getting a good law firm on retainer, and she would start working that angle. Good ole Leah, always thinking one-step ahead for me. Leah also felt that this would be a test for her and Charlie, to see if he would stand beside her through good-times and bad.

"Try not to worry, you will make yourself meshuga," Leah said, "Come home as soon as you can leave town." Leah was worried, it sounded dangerous, if they were finding dead bodies that close to her. Her only consolation was that Eli was nearby and would protect her friend.

When JW approached her car, she saw another note. Carefully opening it she read, 'Bitch I warned you to get out of town, I'm going to kill you. Luther'

This makes my decision about what to do first today. The first stop is the sheriff's office, I need to get on record that psycho has been stalking me, and then I'll go find Charlie and see where we stand.

All the while, she had an eerie feeling that someone was watching her. She looked around her, but saw no one, and very strange feelings gnawed in her gut.

# THIRTY-TWO

Old and pot-bellied Sam Butler had been Sheriff of Grayson County for over 20 years. He knew JW's momma and daddy, and all the skeletons in everyone's closet. He also knew Luther, had arrested him multiple times over the years, and he didn't share her concern over the threatening letter's. Sheriff Butler seemed more concerned about her location than cousin Luther's. She was disappointed when she left the Sheriff's office, that meeting did not go as planned. Once again, he told her not to leave town. She decided to put that worry aside, she needed to go see Charlie.

At the trucking company, she found his truck in the parking lot. She sat in her car and steadied her nerves before going inside. She threw up once in the parking lot, found a breath mint and then entered the front lobby. The receptionist, a cute young girl that looked like she just graduated high school, looked at her sideways. JW had the feeling the word was around town about the fire and the charred body, and that she was probably the prime suspect.

As she waited on Charlie, her eyes took in the room. The furniture in the lobby was high quality walnut hardwoods and top-grain leather seating, nice carpeting and expensive wood paneling. Apparently, Charlie had expensive taste in all aspects of his life, the new dually-wheel truck, the farming equipment, his land holdings, the houseboat, the painting, and his business. From all appearances, his farming and the trucking business must be very profitable, she thought.

Her stomach pitched and gurgled as she waited for Charlie and she hoped she didn't throw-up again. Charlie opened the lobby door and motioned for her to follow him to his private office. He did not smile at her. That is not a good sign, she thought. When they got to his office, he shut the door, and sat on the edge of his massive walnut desk. He lay his cell phone face up so he could monitor the time and incoming calls, crossed his arms across his chest, and glared at her. He was saying nothing with his mouth, but a lot with his actions and body language.

She spoke first, nervously fidgeting with her fingers, "Charlie, we need to talk."

"I'm all ears," he said.

"I am really sorry that I dragged you into this mess, I had no idea there was anyone in the farmhouse…," and she started crying again. "I am so sorry." The tears were sobs now, she was ugly crying, her nose was running and her eye make-up was black and started running down her face, and she stood there looking vulnerable, sad, and broken.

"God, JW, stop crying," he ordered her. "You didn't know there was anyone in that house, did you? Huh, did you?" bullying her to answer.

"No," she said softly and shook her head.

"An accident, right?" He continued, "I'm mad at myself for letting you talk me into something that I should have….shit, what a mess, you've gotten me in." He ran his fingers through his short hair, and she hurt for the pain she caused him.

"All I can do is say I'm sorry. Look, I will tell them it was all my idea, you had nothing to do with it," he interrupted her before she could finish.

"No, you don't talk to anyone, don't say a word, or tell anybody anything. You got that," he said.

He just stood there boring holes through her. He was angry and puffed up, and she hung her head with tears dripping off her face and nose. This went on for what seemed an eternity, then he said, "C'mere," and he held out his hand to her. He had made her suffer enough, he thought. When she moved into his hug, the narcissist Charlie smiled behind her back.

She moved into his arms and the sobs became racking, aching, painful cries, which she could not stop.

He shushed her and ordered, "Don't cry," he pushed her away and looked at his wristwatch. She snuffed and wiped her face on her sleeve, and pulled herself together as best she could. "You go back to the B&B, I'll be in around 6 tonight, and we can talk this out, and try to come up with a plan. OK?" Without waiting for an answer, he started walking her toward the door.

She shook her head yes, and said, "OK, then, I'll see you later." She walked out, crying silently. He walked back to the warehouse, and that was that.

She sat in the parking lot for a while and tried to steady herself, thinking about what just happened. That did not go as she expected either. She left there feeling like she had groveled for his forgiveness, and he did not have an iota of empathy. She had a lot of thinking to do between now and 6 p.m.

She got Eli's phone number from Leah, and they agreed to meet at the truck stop where she had run into Luther earlier in the week. It was on the outskirts of town, and she was less likely to see anyone that might recognize her. She hoped Luther didn't show up again, she didn't think she could take much more stress today.

Eli was still the man dressed in black, and he looked very haggard, she wondered why. She thought the intelligence gathering on Charlie was complete, so she was puzzled he was still in the area. They sat in a booth by the window farthest away from the cash register, talking quietly so the server wouldn't hear them. Sipping black coffees, she talked to Eli about all the problems she was facing, trying not to cry again, and trying to hold herself together.

After unloading all her problems on Eli, he placed his hand over hers on the table and said, "Try not to worry, dear one. This will work out, you did nothing wrong, and it will be alright."

She almost sobbed aloud when she heard his soft reassuring voice. She wondered why didn't Charlie utter those kind words to me, he knows me better than this man does? She had a look of anguish on her face, so Eli continued trying to soothe her with his calm way.

"I have been here for a while, and I will stay to watch as long as you are here. If you ever need me, I am your friend, you may call me," Eli said.

The way he spoke reminded her of Leah. He

exuded kindness and strength, and she felt a peace come over her. She believed him.

He said, "Not everything is always as it seems in life. You must trust me on this, and learn to trust yourself. You are a strong woman, a fighter. You proved that when you tried to defend yourself with a butter knife." He smiled at her. "I see more than you sitting before me. I see the hurt child you once were and the woman you are struggling to become. These two must reconcile within you. Then your soul will be whole, and you will be healed."

She just nodded her head a little, and she tried to believe him.

"I will leave you with these words from the Talmud and then we go, yes? 'Be wary of those who befriend a person for their own purposes. They appear loving when it is beneficial to them, but do not stand by the other person in his time of distress.' I say this to you to remember that your friends will stand by you, always, and I am your friend." He said.

He etched the words on her heart, and her family grew by one more member that day. She felt better when she left him, and knew she would need his friendship for what was looming before her.

Upon returning to the B&B, Sheriff Butler and his deputy were standing on the porch talking with Katie. He waved a piece of paper at her and said, "I have a search warrant here Ma'am, and I'll need to search your room and your car, and all the premises and grounds."

JW went white, and her mind jumped to the burn pile in the field behind house. They will find my boots, then they'll have evidence against me, and I'll be arrested. She would be going to the county jail. She tried to remain stoic, but it was hard to hide her fear. All she could mutter was a weak, "OK." She then punched in Leah's number and said, "Do you have that lawyer on retainer yet, the cops are here with a search warrant?"

Sheriff Butler started in her room, tossed it entirely. She watched with Leah on the cell phone. She whispered into the phone, "Nothing here." When they went back outside her car was being winched onto a flatbed for processing at the State Police Crime Lab. Then they brought out a K9 from the deputy's car. The Sheriff said the dog was trained to alert to arson, blood, and drugs. The dog started energetically working the grounds. He began in a circle around the house and then like a ripple on the water broadened his tracking pattern. She tried not to panic but she knew where the dog's nose was leading it, and what it would find.

"Leah, I'll call you back," she whispered.

The dog went to the burnt spot in the field and sat down, the deputy yelled, "Sheriff, over here. He's alerted to something." They all walked over to a hole in the ground of fresh dirt and looked, puzzled, "What's this deputy?" Sheriff Butler said.

JW looked down at the dirt, she was shocked, and there was nothing there: no burnt clothes, no ashes, no boots, and no nothing….a hole, that's all. She was gulping in air, trying not to be sick and trying not to cry again.

After they were satisfied with their search of the

remaining field, and finding nothing, they loaded the dog, and themselves and prepared to leave empty handed. Once again, he warned her, "don't leave town," as they pulled away.

She went to her room and collapsed on the bed, calling Leah to tell her what had happened. All Leah said was "thank God for Eli."

# THIRTY-THREE

It was nearing 6 p.m. and time for Charlie's arrival at the B&B, so her stomach started heaving bile. Not the reaction you should have when you are preparing to see the love of your life. However, these days were anything but normal. She brushed her teeth and used mint mouthwash to camouflage her weakness, and hoped that his heart had softened since this morning. It was a productive day for her, Leah had secured a New York attorney, and the best money could buy, with reciprocity to a law firm in Louisville. Her legal beagle assured her that 'any time she spent in jail would be minimal', and to say nothing except, 'I want to see my lawyer', when—not if, arrested. Those magic words would cease any interrogation, and they would handle bail—now, how would she deal with Charlie.

He arrived right on time, and with a plan, she felt better. She wasn't in jail for another day, and she decided, no more begging for forgiveness, or for anything. She was done. She did not kill anyone. She did not put a body in the farmhouse. She was done—especially with Charlie's attitude. As soon as she could, she was leaving this place, this time for good. She met him on the front porch with a glass of sweet tea in each hand. Neutral ground she thought, she didn't want him in her bedroom.

"Hi, here," she said handing him a glass. Her

demeanor was as cool as the sweet tea, and composed. She decided to let Charlie take the lead. She had nothing else to say.

Sitting down he blew out a breath of exhaustion, and took a gulp.

"Oh, they towed my car today," she said. "Looking for evidence."

"I heard," he said.

Of course she nodded, Katie tells him everything, probably had him on the phone when the Sheriff was on the porch. But did he come home to help me, nope. Actions speak louder than words she thought.

He twirled the glass in his hand, as if he was more interested in the ice than her and said, "So, I've been thinking all day about this, and I think we ought to get married."

"What? You are proposing to me, here, now, like this. " She said.

"Here me out," he paused, "you know I love you. If this thing gets bad, if we are married, they can't make us testify against each other. Makes a lot of sense," he said.

"I've been doing some thinking today too, and as soon as I get my car back and the all clear, I'm going home," she said. She hoped he realized that no answer was an answer.

Katie called out the door, dinner's ready, but no one seemed to have much of an appetite that evening. It was an early night for everyone with feigned tiredness and each went to their rooms. A heavy funk hung in the air, and no one seemed able to suck in a good, deep breath.

When she was sure that Charlie and Katie were asleep, JW slipped out the back door with a small flashlight she found in the bedside table. She tramped through the mist-laden field, tripping in mole holes and stones hidden in the weeds. She tried not to think about all the critters that came out at night and creepy crawlies that were slithering about in the tall weeds. A few things flushed into the air, some kind of birds—maybe, she hoped. In the trees she saw red night eyes when her light caught them just right. Not sure what those were, she tried not to be afraid, but she was. It took her longer than she figured to get through the rough terrain and to the tree line of cedars at the back of the field. It was no more than 100 yards. She approached a small mound of dirt, with a tuft of tall grass in front of the cedars; she started panning the light from left to right. She found what she was looking for, Eli. He was sitting under the branches of a low hanging cedar tree; he had night glasses in one hand, and a flashlight in the other. A hunting knife strapped to his belt, and he wore a shoulder holster with a very large gun. He sat very still, unsure of what to say, but he had seen her coming.

She spoke first, "I thought you might be out here."

"I have been for a while now," he said. "Home away from home," as he gestured with his hands opening the trees to her.

"Did you see the K9 today?" she asked.

"Oh, yeah, I was up in this very tree, I was worried he might smell me. Shit, I smell me." They both smiled at that remark.

"I think I owe you for taking care of the boots, and the burn pile," she said.

"It's what I do, no thanks needed."

"I'm trying to go home soon and you won't need to babysit me anymore. Can I get you anything?" she cast her eyes downward ashamed at being so needy.

"Like I said, it is what I do, no worries, and I kinda' like watching you."

She nodded toward the house, "I guess I better get back  Maybe tomorrow around 10, I'll take a walk, and I'll sneak you some hot coffee, snacks, OK?"

"That would be lovely, watch your step on the way back, 'nite."

"G'night," she turned the flashlight off and navigated by the light of the moon back to the farmhouse. She certainly did not want Charlie to know about Eli, he would be furious if he found out. Another red flag she thought, keeping secrets from each other, not healthy in a relationship.

Tonight, she dreaded her nightly call to Leah, she felt embarrassed telling her what Charlie had suggested. It was not how she dreamed her bashert would propose.

Shocked by the proposal, Leah said, "very strange." She told JW to come home as soon as she could get away from Hooterville.

"Tomorrow I'm talking to the lawyer about that very thing, I'm ready to leave," JW said.

Preparing for bed her thoughts on Eli—not Charlie, standing vigil, alone in the damp, dark woods, she wanted him warm and safe.

# THIRTY-FOUR

After Charlie left for work the next morning, Katie went to town for groceries; JW gathered a pot of hot coffee in a thermos with her leftover breakfast and headed for the woods.

She retraced her steps from last night, still clearly visible in the tall wet grass. She realized she would never make a very good secret agent, and laughed at her thoughts. Eli was appreciative of the scraps she brought to him, but overjoyed with the hot coffee and elicited M-m-m-m's as he sipped the hot beverage.

She wanted to know how long he had been following her. What other surprises was she in for, and did he know anything about the dead body.

He was evasive with his reply, "you will know all in due time, now is not the time."

She didn't press him and she said, "I have a flight this afternoon, do you need me to book you, or give you a lift?"

"No, I will be right behind you."

After more small talk, she gathered the remnants and hiked back to the farmhouse, carefully cleaning up any evidence in the kitchen. She was centered, calm, and now had a plan. She wondered to herself why after talking to Eli, she always felt better, and after talking to Charlie, she always felt conflicted, sometimes even sad and guilty.

It was no problem for the attorney to get her rental car back from the crime lab, it was clean, and he advised the Sheriff's office she was returning to her home state of New York. They found no evidence against her, yet. She did worry about the gas can; it was clear proof of arson. But, it was consumed in the fire along with fingerprints and any other proof she and Charlie may have shed.

She was booked on the first plane she could find out of town. She didn't even bother to say goodbye to Charlie. He'd call her, or he wouldn't, his loss she thought I'm done crying and apologizing. She flipped her suitcase closed, wheeled it to the car and left Cooper B&B in her rear view mirror, just like the first time on that Greyhound bus. Only this time it was on her terms, she was no longer the scared little girl, and she was flying first class.

Boarding the plane, she surveyed the passengers looking for one in particular. Near the rear of the plane she spotted the familiar face, she pretended not to notice Eli sitting there. He wore a black jacket, over his black t-shirt and jeans. He had showered and shaved, and didn't look like he had been living in the woods for a week or two. After all the passengers boarded, she flagged down the flight attendant and whispered in her ear.

Before the fasten seat belt announcement came over the intercom, Eli appeared beside her and thanked her for his first class upgrade.

"The least I could do, after causing you to live like an animal in the woods for weeks," she said.

The next two hours they spent talking about their

lives, he already knew a great deal about her, she thought Joseph had briefed him before hiring him. She wanted to know about him, his family, his life in Israel, and his work.

Eli spoke five languages fluently: Hebrew, English, Arabic, German, and French, if you counted Yiddish—make that six. He spent his College years at Tel Aviv University, graduating with a 4.0 GPA, in Military Science. They had taught him engineering, psychology, strategic methods and technology, with an emphasis on military tactics, logistics, human behavior, electronics, and biochemistry. After his B.S., he finished his masters at Oxford on full scholarship. Even at his level of performance, he found Oxford intimidating, and not a large Jewish student body. He studied alongside, or sat in the desk where, many of the kings, queens, prince, princesses, and prime ministers of the world will or once sat. His primary goal was not an education, but to build a profile and relationship database to be utilized in his future role with the Mossad. He was successful in both. After returning to Israel, he joined the Mossad Intelligence and he didn't tell her much about what that meant, but he did travel a great deal for work. He had not married, hadn't found the right one yet, but thought he was getting closer. She let that ride.

JW had never met a man like Eli, and she wanted to get to know him better. They shared an Uber from the airport to Joseph and Leah's apartment. She couldn't wait to see her best friend, it had been too long. They usually saw each other every day, and these week's long absences were painful for both of them. Leah hugged them both when they appeared upon her doorstep, laughing about their adventures and starving. Her troubles seemed like a lifetime ago, but they weren't, as she would soon learn.

When Eli and Joseph went to the kitchen, she jerked Leah into the bathroom, flushed the toilet, and turned the faucet on to drown out their conversation. "Leah, we need to talk about Eli," she said as screwed up her lips half-afraid of Leah's response.

"Oy vey, I thought you'd never see him in this way," Leah hugged her friend so tightly, "this would be a wonderful thing, I think." They emerged from the bathroom like two schoolgirls, giggly and holding onto each other.

The men had already made themselves sandwiches and were scarfing them down. Joseph talked between bites, "Eli, is there anything you can tell us about your investigation?"

He looked quizzically at Joseph and said, "Do you think the time is right?"

Joseph tilted his head sideways, bobbled, and raised his hands palm up, "I guess, why not?"

Eli explained that the investigation found some deeper and darker secrets and he called upon some 'associates' to deal with those. He could not talk about that, but he did have some unsettling news for JW.

"Perhaps you should sit down," he took her hand and motioned toward the sofa.

What in the world, she thought. At that very moment her cell phone rang, the attorney that handled the real estate inheritance of the farm.

"Hello," she said.

"Hi, JW, this is Shore and Shore Law in Leitchfield, I also represent a local developer that has negotiated with Charlie Cooper for the 150 acres you acquired from your aunt. My client is concerned that the arson of the farmhouse would slow down the sale. He has a deadline for closing, and has his money together and….."

She interrupted, "What, Charlie sold my land? Remind me, how much did we agreed on?" she tried to be cool and like she knew all about this underhanded act by Charlie.

"The last bid was $32.5K per acre, I think that'd be around five and a quarter million, and that's with you retaining the road frontage and easement across it to the Cooper Farm. I know how important that was to you and Charlie," he said.

"I'm gonna have to give you a call back later this afternoon, something has come up," she nodded, "Yes, I have your number. Just sit tight. Oh, and don't say anything to Charlie about this call, I want to surprise him."

She turned to the three and gave them the other side of the conversation. After she was finished, she put her hands on her hips and calmly said to Eli. "Now, what were you going to tell me?"

Eli proceeded to explain that he had the forensic group at his agency to do a deep dive into Charlie Cooper's financial affairs. What they found was not good. Bank loans were over leveraged on the existing Cooper Family farm, he carried two mortgages—both with past due payments. The farm equipment was financed at over $2.5M, with deficits on the farm income for the last 3 years. The leased land contracts were unpaid and held promissory notes against crop futures, for more than he could clear. The trucking company was deep in the red and creditors were coming out of the woodwork for him. Eli said he didn't know how the guy was juggling all the balls. So, he decided to look deeper, and then he found the answer.

"But, I can't talk about that right now." He said.

She would not cry—she was angry and her voice was stern, "that piece of shit. I was just a mark to him, that's all I was to him? He wanted my land, my money. What about the body in the house, did he have anything to do with that?"

"I can't talk about that right now either," Eli said.

"You don't have to, you just told me. So, what are we going to do about this situation?" She crossed her arms, and sat back trying to comprehend how close she came to utter destruction. She might not be clear yet. Was it his plan all along to frame her for the body, and while she was off serving time, he'd be robbing her blind. She said aloud, "God, what a monster."

While shaking his head, Eli said, "My dear, you only know a small piece of the puzzle, just wait until all is revealed."

"I can hardly wait," she said.

# THIRTY-FIVE

Katie called Charlie as soon as JW's car headed out the driveway, "well, she's gone." That's all she said to him, then, "I gotta go," and she hung up. This whole ordeal tore Katie up; she liked JW, a lot. She and Charlie argued numerous times, about what he was doing to JW, she told him it was wrong. She also knew about Charlie's history with Brenda. She knew he had never stopped seeing that woman, sneaking around late at night with her. Rumors spread around town that her first kid looked an awful lot like a Cooper, Katie didn't doubt it either.

Charlie's debts concerned her too, she knew he was in over his head, but she was powerless to help him. Whenever she tried to talk to him about it, he told her he had it covered. She knew the hanger's-on Charlie ran with in town were unsavory souls. All she could do was watch and worry, and wait to pick him up when he came crashing down. He was still trying so hard to win Daddy's approval and the poor guy never could, and never would.

Meanwhile, later that night and back in her New York apartment, JW waited for her cell phone to ring. She expected Charlie to at least call and say something, my God the man proposed to her last night after all. He hadn't called by 8 p.m., so she thought it won't happen tonight. Then the cell phone rang, it was Charlie's number. She gathered her courage to answer.

She raised the phone to her ear and didn't hear a hello, but a heated argument. Puzzled, she listened hard. She heard Charlie's voice and a woman. She realized it was a butt dial from Charlie. He said the woman's name….. Brenda. Whoa, this is weird. She pressed the record button on her phone, to save the conversation. Crying and screaming Brenda was unleashing hell on Charlie. She heard her name mentioned a couple of times, she couldn't quite make out the context, but it didn't sound good. Brenda told Charlie that she had done everything he asked, she slashed her tires, she left the stalking notes, but she was done. She heard Charlie trying to calm her down, telling her he had a plan all along and it was working. He, no they, needed money and the old farm was worth millions, it was just sitting there for the taking. Once he married JW, and she went to prison for murder, he could do whatever he wanted with the land. They would continue their affair like always. Even when Brenda had been married they had still seen each other, it would be no different with JW. He professed his love to her.

She couldn't listen to any more of their deceit, afraid of being discovered, she disconnected. Her heart hurt, and she vomited, but she would not cry over him anymore. She had come so close to falling for the lie's he spewed. Plain and simple, he was a narcissist, a manipulator, and a very good one. Once again, a person that promised to take care of her had let her down. He used her, deceived her, and came close to destroying her life, a life she had worked so hard to make for herself.

She needed a break, and her marble-jetted tub called her name for a long hot soak. It had been a long and exhausting day. She found a bag of magnesium bath flakes in her linen closet, and noticed it came from the salt lake from the Dead Sea in Israel. She never noticed that until tonight, how ironic. She had to tell Eli that next time she talked to him. He popped into her head; she wanted to talk with him. He was easy to be with, a gentle soul, he resonated safety to her, and he was like a warm bath— soothing.

As she soaked her aches away, she pondered how best to deal with Charlie, when he called. He will call; he won't let his easy mark get away. Probably start with flowers, then text, then phone calls. She had the upper hand for now, he did not know about the call from the developer, or that she knew about his affair with Brenda. So, how should she play her cards? Does she go with the flow and see how far he leads her on, or does she call him on his game and let him know the gig is up. She might need him; he is the only one that knows what really happened the night of the fire, but would he tell the truth if she needed him to. Like momma always said and she whispered aloud to herself, "you play with a snake, you're gonna get bit."

It was the next morning when Charlie made the first attempt to reach her. Around 10 a.m. he called, she didn't answer. He left a painful message, about how sorry he was, how much he missed her and he needed a 'do-over'. She was disgusted, but she saved the message.

Around noon, the bouquet of flowers arrived. They were beautiful sunflowers and wildflowers with a very sweet note, apologizing and asking her to please call. He needed her. Damn right, she thought, he needs my money. She got angrier.

Then promptly at 2 p.m., the first text came in. More of the same, miss you, love you, can't live without you, please forgive me, please come back to me. Yadda, yadda, yadda, she thought.

She called Leah, shared the sordid mess from last night until the latest texting, "so, my dear, what to do?"

"I kinda like you stringing him along, play dumb as he thinks you are, why not?" Leah said.

"That's what my gut was telling me too, you know my gut has been right all along with this guy," she said. She wanted to tell Eli, what was happening and make sure he agreed with the plan. She also, wanted to hear his voice.

"Come for dinner, Eli's here for a while longer; I'll make my roasted lemon-pepper chicken, you know it is to die for, be here at six," Leah said.

She looked forward to her dinner plans the rest of the day, and not just for Leah's delicious roast chicken. A force of nature beyond explanation pulled her towards Eli, like bees to nectar. She got excited to know she was seeing him again tonight. It made her happy. Eli emitted an invisible force that drew her towards him. She felt an attraction and was unable to shield herself, she didn't want to either.

# THIRTY-SIX

For once in her life, she was early for a dinner date. She could hardly wait to see Eli, Leah, and Joseph, even though she had just been with them last night. As usual, she knocked on their door, and then let herself in as if she belonged there, because she did. She greeted everyone with hugs all around. As she hugged Eli, and then released him, she wondered. Did he linger a bit longer and a hug a tad tighter than the others did, or was her imagination working overtime?

Dinner was delicious, and the favorite part of the evening was at hand—the deep conversation amongst good friends. They would talk about whatever entered their minds, except work. The trio established a rule early on in the business relationship they would not talk shop at home.

JW's troubles were on everyone's minds and were a prime topic on the table for discussion tonight. She shared with Eli and Joseph details of the butt-dial from Brenda and Charlie. It would be funny, if it weren't so awful.

"So, Charlie proved to be a snake in the grass?" Eli said.

"Yes, my momma once warned me about playing with snakes," she said.

They glanced at each other and she caught Eli's eyes with hers. She could not break away from his gaze, eyes so brown they looked bottomless. She felt like an intruder that was looking into his soul, without an invitation. He was fully open to her intrusion, accepting, inviting, as if they were the only two in the room. She liked where this was going.

"Earth to JW, earth to JW," Leah said.

She blushed and cleared her throat, "Yeah, what?"

Leah and Joseph cackled with laughter.

Eli spoke to relieve the awkwardness after taking a sip of coffee, "I heard from an associate today about our problem in Kentucky."

"Share what you know, now," JW said.

"The State Crime Lab ID'd the body, as Luther Walker. They ruled death by homicide."

JW shook her head when she heard the word homicide and her cousin's name. She felt the room wobble, and the familiar stomach lurch.

He patted her hand to calm her, and continued, "They matched DNA, his was in the system from priors," Eli said. He took a bite of pie and while chewing said, "U-m-m-m, this is good, the tox screen showed multiple drugs and alcohol on board, also found a linear wound on the pulmonary artery and aorta. Murder weapon was a 16" smooth one-side, saw tooth other-side blade, like a Bowie knife. Killer knew how to use it too. Lungs were clear, supports theory that he was murdered and dumped before the fire. There was evidence of an old skull fracture, recent but healing breaks on one arm and right knee and broken ribs." He spoke in clipped sentences and he looked directly at JW. "You were set-up to be framed for murder."

He continued, "There was only one person other than you that knew you were going to burn that house that night, and that was Charlie. The murder weapon fits the description of a Marine standard issue Ranger knife.

"Oh," he stopped talking to take another bite, and then said, "and I also happen to have a video of the whole thing."

"You what," she paused open-mouthed. "You let me go through a living hell this whole time, and you have a video."

He took another bite of pie and said, "I'm sorry. But, you are now vindicated."

He described what was captured on the video, "Charlie bought the gas can, gasoline, lured Luther to the farmhouse, gave him booze and drugs, and stabbed him. Took him out on the front porch, gutted him like a fish, and dumped him in the back room. You came along and torched the place. C'est voila."

She loved it when he spoke French, even in the context of murder. Weird she thought.

"So, what should I do now?" She asked.

"Nothing yet my dear, there is more to come, which will play out," he said.

All she heard, was Eli calling her dear, this conversation gets weirder by the minute. What is wrong with me, she thought and shook her head to clear it.

Joseph piped in, "So, do we need to get her lawyer up to speed, or what?"

"You are no longer under suspicion for this, that's

not 'official', but it looks too professional to them. This whole thing goes much deeper and it will all become clear in the end. You do nothing," speaking directly to JW.

Eli raised his cup of coffee like a toast and said, "Let's talk about, art, and love and forget about this Charlie and his mess, shall we?"

For the first time in a long time, she was relieved, she said, "Eli, you're awesome. Would it be corny to say, you're my hero." She raised her cup to toast him too."

The evening ended too soon for JW. Eli walked her the few blocks to her apartment and as she was unlocking her door, she asked, "Would you like to come in for a nightcap?"

"I'm sorry, but the Talmud forbids being alone or touching the opposite sex, before marriage. This creates one mind and a strong foundation for marriage," he said.

He looked deep into her eyes, trying to see if she agreed and then continued, "The mind should lead the heart, and not the other way around, a man must find favor in his beloved's eyes." She looked down when he said this for it was too intense.

"We believe sexual attraction is a sacred calling of the soul and intimacy is a spiritual experience. I would very much like to get to know you better," he cast his eyes downward and his voice was nervous.

"I would be honored," she said.

"Don't laugh when I tell you that most dates happen at the airport," he said.

"Why there?" She asked.

"It is a very public place, easy to get to, lots of places to sit and talk, and a food court. So, would you like to go to LaGuardia with me?" He smiled as he asked her.

"I would be delighted," and they made a very unusual date for the next day.

She shut the door softly, and then she danced around the room. JW could hardly wait to call Leah, she was worried that the news might be met with resistance, but it wasn't. Leah and Joseph had been hoping for this all along.

# THIRTY-SEVEN

Eli met her in front of her apartment building, and they Ubered to LaGuardia. The driver was surprised that they had no luggage. They agreed to go Dutch treat, Eli would pay one way, and JW would pay the return. She liked that, equal partners.

After thinking about this meeting since yesterday, she decided to undertake it as an experiment, no expectations, and to live in the moment. "Carpe Diem," she said. An added bonus, this would make a great story for her future kids and grandkids—if she ever had any. After trying secular dating, most recently with 'Charlie the snake', she figured she had nothing to lose.

She was unsure how to go about an airport meeting, so she would follow Eli's lead. One thing she noticed around Eli, her stomach never betrayed her. No lurching, no vomiting, this was promising.

The Uber dropped them at departing flights entrance, and they rode the escalator to the upper level. With seats facing each other, in the center of the atrium with the least foot traffic, she said, "I have no idea what to do here." She was clicking her fingernails of one hand on the other, like the clacking of a typewriter.

"Simple, we just talk, get to know one another," he knew she was nervous and he said, "don't be nervous, it's just me. I want to know your dreams and desires. Because I don't know if I could ever keep up with you."

She was floored, "I've never had anyone ask me about my dreams before, I think I might cry."

Laughing he said, "Please, I can't make you cry on our first meeting, that usually doesn't happen until much later."

JW sat back, got comfortable in her seat, looked off into her future, and started dreaming, as if she was talking to herself. After a while, their stomachs started growling, and they walked to nearby deli in the food court. The conversation continued over food. Eli described what living with an Israeli, maybe even in Israel, would be like. They would be a Jewish family; faith was a part of his life and would be the foundation of their home.

He didn't waste any time. She often dreamed of a home with a family and children, but did not believe it would ever happen for her. Could it be? She was already 35 and her eggs were getting stale, if they wanted babies they would need to move fast. JW was ready to embrace her faith, was Eli her missing other half—her bashert?

Eli told her of his dreams and desires for the future. When he spoke of his hope to have a family, she almost swooned. His faith tells him that God has created his wife for him and the bond with his wife to be like no other relationship. He believes that marriage is intimate and holy. He longs to be a husband and a father. To raise his children to grow into good and kind people, he would raise them to be good people and follow the 'mitzvah'—this is a commandment of Jewish law, good deeds, acts of empathy and kindness. He valued his God, family, faithfulness, education, the arts, the sciences, happiness, and laughter.

"God joins us in marriage by our souls, 'Neshama', in heaven, and we must find our other half on earth. Are you my other half?" He asked softly, looking deep into her eyes to find the answer written there.

After they shared their hearts, there was only one more thing she needed to tell him. Could he deal with her intimacy issues? Would he help her to overcome them, or would he get angry when she had flashbacks and froze? She would save this for a future discussion; she wanted to see if he still was interested after peering into her soul tonight.

The airport foot traffic slowed, and when they checked the time, they realized it was already 9 p.m. Time to Uber them from the future, back to current day Manhattan. They stopped in to visit Leah and Joseph on the way home.

JW wasn't sure what to share with Leah, so she decided to say nothing yet. Joseph opened a bottle of merlot. They sat in the comfortable living room laughing easily and just being together. Strangely, Leah refused wine, and drank bottled water. She loves wine, what gives, JW wondered. Maybe she's not feeling well; I'll ask her about that tomorrow in private.

Tomorrow was a workday; she needed to finish the piece that was in the studio. Eli needed to know more about what she did for a living too. Her art was not just a job, but it was part of her life. They needed to know how this would affect their future lives together.

So, she decided to ask him, "Eli, I need to work in the studio tomorrow, would you like to come by and check it out?"

"That would be awesome; I have such admiration for artist. I don't have a creative bone in my body. What time?"

"Come to the back door around 10, I'll be waiting for you." She said.

She was giddy when she got home and couldn't sleep. She could not stop thinking about Eli and imagining the future life, he described. She wanted that life too.

The best part of the evening was when he agreed to come to her studio tomorrow. This would be a true test, for her art was a part of her, without it she could not live.

They had not shared the first dance, first kiss, or even held hands yet and she was counting the hours until they could be together again. This was very strange process to her, but she found it titillating. He made her insides quiver when he drew near her. It started in her belly and inched upwards into her chest. It was not painful, but it quickened and sometimes she had trouble breathing normally. She felt sparks shoot from her fingertips, when his hands came near hers, but of course, no one could see this but her.

When Eli spoke, he had a slight accent and used his hands a lot. He was animated and excited and she hungered for more stories of his world travels. He had a unique perspective on the simplest things that opened her eyes to new ideas and she wanted more of Eli, much more.

# THIRTY-EIGHT

Promptly at ten Eli knocked on the back door of the gallery. JW had been working for a couple of hours and counting the minutes until Eli showed up. She was nervous, but excited. He brought her a coffee from the little barista on the corner, hot and black. Impressed that he remembered how she took it.

He was shocked taking in the massive canvas screwed to the wall and saw that she had a stepladder positioned so she could reach the top. This was an unusually large and difficult piece. But, she didn't choose the canvas or the painting, they chose her. As an artist, she would look at the white space before her, and shapes and forms would start to appear, she just filled in the blanks. That was her process, and this canvas proved no exception. It was dark and swirling and felt strangely like her life was for the past couple of months. She was applying the finishing varnish to seal the canvas.

After a private studio tour for Eli, she escorted him through the gallery. Her work still hanging from the solo show and Eli was awestruck. He paused before several of her pieces, noted all the sold labels, and said numerous times, "I really like this one." Each time it elicited a smile from her, and it took them two hours to walk through the exhibit. They took their sweet time reveling in the solitude of the gallery, their time together, the smell of the dried paint and varnish and easy comfort with one another. He questioned her creative process, trying to find out where the 'secret sauce' comes from.

He asked the same thing most people ask, "Where do your ideas come from?" She gave the usual cliché answer, "why the idea mart, of course." Of course, the truth is artists have no idea how it happens or what makes the creative juices flow, it just happens. Writers write the movie that is playing in their head, artist paint the colors and shapes they see in their minds eye before they are real. It is a beautiful mystery every time, to the artist as well.

She asked a tough question that had been nagging at her, "Eli, if we have a future together, can you accept me continuing my work, my career? I need my art to breath; it is a part of me. I can't give it up."

"Oh my dear, how could you ever give this up? This is a gift from God and its, its otherworldly. One should not stifle a gift that would be like telling Michelangelo not to paint or sculpt. I would never do that, to take God's blessing from you, never."

He watched as she climbed the ladder to go back to work; she eventually forgot he was there. He was mesmerized with her. Finally, he said, "I need to go take care of some paperwork, how about we meet at Leah's tonight, around six?"

"I'd like that, I'll see you then. Can you find your way out?" She said without looking at him, totally absorbed in the canvas.

He turned to go and hesitated, he had trouble leaving her more and more.

She worked until a text message pinged. It was the attorney about the farmland, wanting to know if she wanted him to handle the real estate transaction. She gave him a call and authorized the sale, but she wanted the graves surveyed into a perpetual plot and protected as a final resting place for her parents and aunt and uncle's, and she wanted to retain five acres of property with road frontage. They agreed on a closing date, and she would come down in person to sign the papers. She wanted Leah, Joseph, and Eli to go with her to say goodbye to her birthplace, finalize the graveyard, and reveal her plans for the five acres.

She would round up the troops tonight and get them to agree to go with her. She knew they would. She could hardly wait to see Eli again tonight he was growing on her.

She arrived promptly at six for dinner and everyone was shocked that she was on time again, for she was never on time. The menu was a hearty stew, an Israeli goulash, with fresh baked bread, the aroma of the bread hung in the air. She could almost taste the meal with her nose. The spices in the stew were what made the dish special. Leah's goulash was a recipe handed down from Mother Wasserman; it featured select beef tips, potatoes, carrots, tomatoes, garlic and bell peppers all seasoned with 'Baharat' spice mixture. These spices, a combination of black peppercorns, cardamom, cloves, cumin, allspice, turmeric, saffron, ginger, paprika, chili, and coriander, infuse the dish with that special flavor. JW was seeing a new side of Leah too. She was becoming 'homey', cooking, baking, what gives with that she thought?

After dinner while serving coffee and apple pie rugelach, which was to die for, JW broke the news about selling the farm and asking them to go with her back to Kentucky. Leah was hesitant, she had memories of the skinhead at the town square, but if Eli and Joseph went, she was all in. They agreed not to stay at the B&B, and to keep their distance from Charlie. After finalizing the trip, they got down to business of discussing life.

Eli shared what life is like in Tel Aviv, day trips to the beach and floating in the hypersaline Dead Sea. He regaled her with tales of learning to swim— floating in water ten times saltier than the ocean, of how in the dusk of the evening he picked ripe olives from the family garden in the back yard for dinner, and laughing at stories of his family. JW began to fall in love with Israel and the thought of having a big family to share. She tried to imagine her life with this man and she wanted more of Eli.

Joseph also shared stories of growing up with his cousin. He had stayed with family in Tel Aviv, and Eli had spent many summers in New York with him, they were close as brothers. They seemed so much alike and she wondered why she had never met Eli before. She had envied Leah's marriage to Joseph for many years. She didn't think there was anyone else out there like him. Good men are hard to find, she thought, yet here was Eli living and breathing, and telling amazing stories right in front of her.

After the pleasantries of the evening, Eli said, "I have the dossier prepared on Charlie, how do you want the information?" He looked back and forth from Joseph to JW for an answer.

"Now is good as time as any," Joseph answered.

Eli explained his methodology and surveillance on Charlie, how he had 'the office' do the background records of military service, and he performed on-the-ground recon. What he found was very interesting.

He went on, "First of all, we found that Charlie did not graduate from Texas A&M. He only went one year, flunked out, and then joined the Marines in 2002. He did complete the Marine Ranger Scout Sniper program and graduated, that's a tough thing to do. A Marine Scout Sniper is a bad dude; they actually brand them over the heart when they complete the program, a tiny SS." JW recalled the scar she had traced on his chest with her fingertips. Eli kept talking, "They are highly recruited once they come out of service. Most end up as cops, or secret service, CIA or do as Charlie did and go into paramilitary security consulting. That's where the money is to be made, all offshore, tax exempt and good money. So, after his initial tour in Afghanistan and his four years were up," He segued, "and that's where this got interesting," he paused. "Do you remember the Blackwater incident in Iraq?" He stopped and sipped his coffee, not expecting an answer before continuing. "The Iraqi's call it the Nisour Square massacre; we call it 'Blackwater'. Blackwater was hired to escort a U.S. embassy convoy, and it was claimed they shot at Iraqi civilians, killed seven, and wounded twenty. Of course, Iraqi says unprovoked, Blackwater says they responded in kind. It's my understanding, some civilians failed to stop at a roundabout and the security team proceeded to fire on the approaching car. Killed were a man and his mother driving a Kia and an Iraqi police officer directing traffic. Then all hell broke loose, it was a bloodbath. Shots were whizzing all around; both sides thought they were under attack. The U.S. security was shooting anything that moved. Only way, it stopped was when another security man put a gun to the shooters head and ordered him to stop firing. Our boy Charlie was the shooter. He did some time awaiting trial, he was not convicted, but others were and when he was free he returned to Kentucky."

"Oh my gosh, that's horrible," JW was moved to tears. She wasn't sure how to feel, bad for Charlie, or sad for innocent victims. Were they innocent victims or insurgents, it was too much to comprehend. So she just sat still trying to make sense of a war and a hard world, and a broken man that returned to a Kentucky home.

Eli continued, "Then we move to current day, he's got a lot of debt, no money to pay that debt, so he gets creative. He starts a trucking company, specializes in logistics from Mexico and Latin America. There is more to this story, but I can't talk about that just yet. But, JW you were setup to be a quick payout. He saw the opportunity to marry you and frame you for murder. By killing Luther, he was rid of a talkative witness and set you up in one fell swoop. He would have control of all your assets, immediately increasing his cash flow. I am truly sorry to tell you this."

Shaking JW said, "I knew he was moving awfully fast for some reason. Thank God, I trusted my gut. You know there has been nothing but hurt for me in that town. I plan to change that. Let's get off this subject, its unpleasant. Tell me more about Israel, Eli."

# THIRTY-NINE

The four of them boarded the plane for Louisville; this was to be a fun trip too. It would be Joseph's first time in Kentucky. Before they ventured on to Leitchfield, they wanted to sightsee in Louisville, known for 'beautiful horses, fast women and the bourbon trail'. The day started at Churchill Downs, with the luscious flower laden gardens, the Twin Spires, and thoroughbreds bred and born to run. They caught some races, won a few, lost a few, and the men smoked some stogies. JW tried her first and last mint julep, not the drink for her.

The following day, they toured downtown Louisville sites, visiting the Muhammad Ali Museum, and the Louisville Slugger Museum and Bat Factory—home to the #1 bat used in major league baseball and a 120' bat in front of the building. The day ended with dinner at Proof on Main, a top 5 star restaurant, with the attached 21C museum hotel. As they dined, contemporary art surrounded them on the walls. However, the most unusual thing about the restaurant was the men's restroom, where the urinals are a trench in the concrete floor, which face a one-way mirror. You can see people walking by as you stand there and relieve yourself, kind of freaky. After the men shared this tidbit, Leah and JW had to go into the restroom and check it out, while the men guarded the door.

Named the Bourbon Capital of the World, Louisville they decided to take the Bourbon Trail Tour. There were over 37 or more distilleries in the area, so the group decided to try only three of them. They were not much on sampling hard spirits but wanted to see the manufacturing and bottling process. The most famous distillery was Maker's Mark, the bottle with the dripping red wax seal on the top, and they opted for the immersion package and dipped their own bottle in the hot wax for a special souvenir.

The following day it was on to Leitchfield for the closing on the property. Before going to the attorney's office, the group drove to the old farmhouse. The rubble from the fire was still there. Some sidewalls remained, two-by-fours stood hauntingly in the air, jutting up like rib cages not consumed in the crematory. Old yellow and black crime scene tape was fluttering in the wind around the big maple tree in the front yard. It was an eerie site in the bright sunlight, but the menacing rooms were no more. Oddly, JW's spirit felt released by seeing the ashes.

Eli said as he walked around the debris, "Hell of a message you sent. Remind me never to piss you off, ok?"

JW chuckled at that, she felt empowered, and she was healing.

They all walked behind the house, where the graves were located. There were surveyor flags around the four corners, marking the boundaries of her family cemetery. JW would set up an association to legally protect the graves, and fund upkeep in perpetuity. There were also stakes driven into the ground along the road leading into the driveway, for the five acres she kept. There was still a lot of work to do before announcing the plan for this land. All in due time, she thought. It will be a surprise.

She signed the paperwork and the money wired into JW's account immediately. She was relieved to be rid of it, and laughed when she said, "Dinner's on me tonight. We can do Cracker Barrel, or the Steak House." They chose the steak house, and after dinner, they sat around the lobby of the Best Western and continued their good times together. Eli broke into the conversation around ten and said, "If you all want to see some excitement tonight, we can take a field trip around eleven. Guarantee you won't want to miss this JW."

"I'm game for anything with you," she said.

"Dress in all black, with jackets, and meet me in the lobby at 10:45 p.m., I'll drive," Eli said.

They piled into the rented black SUV rental, a perfect car for a caper JW thought. A few minutes later, they were near Charlie's Trucking Company, but a field separated them from the back of the building. They walked across the field quietly and quickly, and lay down on the ground in a ditch with their heads popping up like whack-a-moles. They had a prime view of the loading docks, where the big trucks backed their trailers into the slots against the building to be unloaded with forklifts. The bays were brightly lit, but not many workers, maybe one, or two. She saw Charlie standing on the dock talking to one of the drivers. He looked intimidating even from this far away. They watched and at midnight on the dot, the place lit up. State police cars with lights flashing roared through the gates, along with several black vans. The doors flew open and out jumped officers dressed in swat gear with 'FBI and DEA' agents stamped in large yellow block letters on their backs and chest. A helicopter hovered overhead with bright spotlights shining on building, the dust, and debris flying in the air. K9 dogs and handlers started working their magic noses on the trailers, and trucks. The agents stormed the building and shouted at Charlie and the others down on the ground. After cuffing him, they placed him into the backseat of the state police cruiser. The agents then brought out tools from the van and started dismantling the trailer, stacking bricks of white on skids in the middle of the parking lot. They dismantled the entire truck in short order, then on to the next one and the next one. JW watched them tear apart four, and load up the bricks onto the skids.

"If that's what I think it is, that's a lot of coke," JW said.

Eli said, "You would be correct."

They watched the show and eventually, Eli told them to wait there, do not move as he approached one of the agents in the parking lot. They looked like they knew each other and shook hands, and slaps on each other's backs. Eli pointed toward the ditch, and the agent shook his head ok, Eli waved the group over. They approach apprehensively, and made sure they stood next to Eli quickly. He introduced JW as

Charlie's vic and said a few other things she could not hear. The agent shook his head and mumbled something like sorry and said, "Sure." They led Eli and JW to the car that housed Charlie, the others followed. The agent rolled his rear window down, and said "Charlie, my man, you've got visitors." Charlie peered out into the night with anger written on his face. His eyes were white wild.

Eli started first, "Hey Charlie, you don't look like you're doing too well tonight. I brought JW to watch you go down, thanks for a great show—only fitting since you tried to frame her for murder." Then he turned to JW and said, "You want to say something?"

She turned to face Charlie, "I'm not sure what to say to you. How could you do these things?"

Charlie shouted at her, until spittle flew out, "You snooty bitch, you don't have a clue what I've been through, in Afghanistan. That's nothing compared to what I had to do, and for what, I got nothing. JW, you were nothing but collateral damage to me, a means to an end."

She refused to cry, she stood proud and tall and stuck out her chest and said, "don't ever call me JW anymore." She shouted, "I am WANDA JANE, and I am not a victim anymore, I am a survivor, and I will protect her and claim what is hers. I am not running away anymore."

Eli wrapped his strong arm around her shoulders. Leah beamed with pride at her friends and all she could think was, boy they are a handsome-looking couple.

On the way back to the hotel, Eli told them how

he had uncovered the smuggling ring. The skinhead he had interrogated told him everything; he was an intermediary that helped Charlie move the dope. He used the skinheads, and a motorcycle gang for distribution. Charlie collaborated with the Mexican cartel to get the goods, transported it on his trucks. He bribed guards, when he could or smuggled to get it through the border and into his dock. The distribution spanned out like spokes on a wagon wheel from Kentucky, to the East coast, and up I65 into Chicago and Michigan, and west to Missouri.

Eli elaborated, "Luther got in the way, and he was demanding more money from Charlie. He was of no value, had a big mouth, and his death was a way to get JW framed for murder. A couple of problems disrupted Charlie's plan though. I moved your boots from the field, which had gas and blood on them from the fire. Charlie tipped the Sheriff to look at you and Okayed the search, when they didn't find any evidence, they couldn't tie you to the murder. From staking out Charlie, I saw him dump his clothes, boots, and the murder weapon. I sent it to my friends at the FBI and DEA. It had Charlie and Luther's DNA all over it, and Luther's blood on the knife; I included a video of the murder, and Charlie unloading Coke shipments, and tied a neat bow on it. Bye-bye Charlie.

JW said, "Eli, I owe you my life, I could have been killed or framed and in prison for life. I don't know how to thank you."

He smiled and said quietly, "I have some ideas. We can talk about that later."

# FORTY

Six months had passed since Charlie's arrest, and their adventure in Kentucky. A colorful fall and cold deep winter had come and gone. An early spring was in the air, Central Park was in bloom, and rebirth and renewal was in the air.

Eli heard from his associates that Charlie had taken a plea deal for reduced charges in return for his testimony. There was no trial, he pled guilty to murder and trafficking in controlled substances under the RICO Act, as a trade to take the death penalty off the table for Luther's murder. The evidence was overwhelming against him; they had DNA and Luther's blood on his clothes, fingerprints on the murder weapon, and video of the stabbing and drug trafficking.

He received a life sentence and assigned to the high security United States Penitentiary Florence, Colorado. This is the most restrictive facility in the federal prison system, and a federal supermax, which holds inmates considered the most dangerous and in need of the tightest controls and confined to a 7' x 12' single cell 23 hours per day and monitored for 24. The cells have one window 4" x 4' tall, and inmates can only see the sky and roof. Their exercise yard is a concrete pit, like an empty swimming pool, large enough for one prisoner to walk 10 steps in a straight line or 31 steps in a circle. This high security facility has secure perimeters with reinforced fences and the highest staff to inmate ratio, and is for inmates most capable of extreme, sustained violence toward staff or other inmates. To win a stay at a supermax, the Bureau of Prisons use the offender classification system, and score inmates according to the level of security risk. Charlie had been ranked 'high risk' since he was classified into the 'Greatest Severity Offense' range. He garnered this ranking because he was a trained killer, and had committed arson, homicide, large-scale drug activities, and had affiliation with a 'disruptive group'—skinheads and motorcycle gangs. This rating and level of confinement is for the worst of the worst.

His troubles did not end with a prison sentence alone since they auctioned the farm, business, and all his toys to pay the creditors. Katie had been able to hold on to the farmhouse and 20 acres, and she still runs it as a B&B. She didn't know anything about Charlie's illegal activities. Brenda Johnson married Charlie while in prison, and she moved close to his prison so she could visit. She gets up to five visits per month, and can kiss upon arriving and leaving, unfortunately, there are no conjugal visits allowed.

Eli, JW, Leah, and Joseph had continued to spend time together over the fall and winter, and their friendship, faith, and love deepened.

Eli and JW became inseparable; she had been attending the synagogue with him, and had many sessions with rabbi about conversion to the faith. Tonight JW was hosting Shabbat dinner for all of them at her apartment. Shabbat was the beginning of the Sabbath. It was the transition period from everyday life into a spiritual time. JW had set the dinner table with her finest china, and candles were ready for lighting. She had baked challah bread with a braided top and it glistened from the egg wash she had lovingly applied, she had become quite accomplished in the kitchen. For tonight's intro course, she had made chicken soup with matzo balls. She prepared Matzo balls with matzo meal and eggs, water and oil, and she served them along with an herb baked chicken and roasted vegetables. For desert, Leah was bringing a surprise from the local kosher bakery.

Eli was selecting a fine red wine and when they were all together, he would then light the candles to start dinner. After which they sing, to welcome the angels of Shabbat to their table. They would start with a blessing said over the wine and then a blessing said over the challah bread. During dinner, there would be lots of talking, laughing, and eating. Followed by another blessing after the meal was finished. The rest of the evening was for visiting, talking, and enjoying the family time together.

Joseph and Eli were like brothers and had spent many summers in New York growing up together, and their funny stories were endless. They seemed so much alike and she wondered why she had never met Eli earlier, she realized she had not been looking. He had been at Joseph's wedding, she never noticed, she was too broken and too focused on her career. For years, she had envied Leah and Joseph's marriage and home, she longed for that type of relationship. She didn't believe there was anyone else out there like him. Good men are hard to find, yet, she found one. Eli was real, living, and breathing, and telling amazing stories right in front of her. She needed to pinch herself. Instead, she whispered for Leah to meet her in the kitchen.

Alone in the kitchen, JW grabbed Leah's elbow and whispered into her ear, "so, this is getting serious, what are your thoughts on me and Eli as a couple?"

Leah put her arms around JW's neck and hugged her so tight, "Eli is such a mensch, and you two would be awesome together."

"When you go back in there, tell Joseph to come help me in the kitchen," she winked as she said this to JW. She was trying to give Eli time alone with her, without breaking rules.

JW relayed the message to Joseph and took a seat at the end of the sofa, nearest Eli's chair. He looked at her and said, "I'm glad we are together for a moment. I've been thinking a lot about something." He had a napkin in his hand and he was twirling the end around his finger nervously.

She was worried but smiled, "Yeah?"

"We have not known each other for very long, but I do know you. I recognized my other half the first time I saw you. It is you—you are my bashert. You are my destiny." He cleared his throat and said, "JW will you be my wife? I promise I will give you the desires of your heart. For I loved you yesterday, I love you today, and I will love you for all eternity."

She had not expected this to happen tonight, for

months, they had been discussing a life together, but this was a surprise. Her heart exploded at the thought of marrying Eli and starting their own family together. She had longed for a relationship like Leah and Joseph had for so many years, but didn't think she would ever find her perfect half. She genuinely loved this man with her mind and her heart, and they had been through so much together. She was open and honest with him, he knew her past and her desires for the future, and there were no secrets. They were friends first, equals in life and now she would have the love she had craved.

"Oh, Eli, Yes, yes, yes."

He knelt before her and took her left hand and gently lifted it to his lips, and kissed the back of it so tenderly, then ran his fingertips down the side of her face, tracing her jawline. "You are so beautiful, inside and out. You've made me the happiest man tonight, and I shall love you like no other, you have my promise on this."

She heard Leah yelp with happiness in the kitchen, and then come running back into the room to hug her. She said, "Yes, we are getting married, finally."

The rest of the evening was a blur, as was the next six months. They planned to get married in Israel where most of Eli's relatives and friends lived and worked. She had no living relatives and her friends were Leah and Joseph's friends, and the Wasserman family. They all agreed to return to Tel Aviv for the wedding. It was to be a traditional Jewish ceremony, and she could hardly wait until she and Eli could be together as one.

She told him about the abuse and the flashbacks she suffered from sometimes. He told her that he would be patient and loving and when the time came, they would work through it together no matter how long it took. He was a patient man, and she was worthy of the wait. Even if never resolved, he would love her like no other. He did want to have children and a family of their own, she did too with all her heart, and together they would heal. He believed together they would overcome.

The wedding was held in Tel Aviv; she met and married into Eli's family in one glorious weekend event. A Jewish wedding is a party and it last until the early morning hours. Eli prepared the Ketubah, or marriage contract, and Leah and Joseph signed as witnesses. He read it to the guest during the ceremony, and then Eli placed her veil over her face as tradition calls. Eli's parents walked him down the aisle to the chuppah; the four corners of the chuppah symbolize the new home they are building together. JW followed with Leah and Joseph since she had no parents and they all stood with them under the altar covering. JW circled seven times around Eli symbolically creating a new family circle. They exchanged simple pure gold wedding bands. The seven blessings were shared from friends and family in the congregation, and then afterward a glass wrapped in a towel was stepped on by Eli to represent the commitment to stand by one another even in hard times, and the shards of glass are collected and saved as a memory. 'Mazel Tov' rang out, as soon as the glass was broken,

Her favorite part of the ceremony was the Yichud, which is the eight minutes of seclusion the newly married share together alone right after the ceremony. This was the first kiss shared between the beloveds. Alone and in the sequestered backroom, Eli lifted her veil, looked deep into her glistening eyes, and embraced her with his strong arms. Their lips met, tentatively at first, and then the fire erupted between them. He kissed as good as he looked, and she melted into him. Her passion burned and she felt him respond to her body with his. He pulled away, not because he wanted too, but he needed too since they still had a lot of wedding celebration to do before the consummation.

Their guest feasted on a sumptuous meal, and a DJ played for hours, at one point the couple sat in chairs and were lifted into the air while each holding onto a cloth napkins and everyone danced the hora in a circle around them. The party continued until the early hours of the next day.

In the wee hours of the morning, they collapsed in their bed at the hotel near the synagogue; they were too tired for romance. The real honeymoon was to be in the southern part, Ein Bokek area, and is the lowest settlement in the world. A two-hour drive from Tel Aviv and east of Jerusalem, when they checked into their hotel it was early afternoon. JW opened the terrace door and walked out onto the balcony to see the water. It was all she had imagined in her mind.

The Dead Sea is actually not a sea, but a lake with an extremely high salt content. The ocean's salt content is about 3.5%, the Dead Sea is over 33% salt, Eli warned her how dangerous it was to enter the salty water. No splashing, no running, and he cautioned her to float on her back that it was very difficult to turn over in the hypersaline water, and get her head under the surface. Ingesting a small amount of this water can be fatal and it is nearly impossible to swim in it because it is so dense. It is actually very dangerous.

They walked down to the shore and she was surprised to see the salt formations on the water's edge, with a deep, uneven, white crust everywhere. It was apparent, there was no life in the water, and she waded cautiously out, until waist high with her sandals still on her feet. The water was not like water at all, it was oily. She lay back cautiously with Eli at her side to help her if she needed him. The water was so buoyant, unlike any experience she ever had before, she just floated as a leaf on the gentle breeze, effortlessly and timeless.

After a short float and exploration of the area, they went back to the room and showered the salt off their bodies. She definitely need moisturized after that experience, so she took the bottle of lotion to the bedroom. Eli had already showered and lay wrapped in a towel from the waist down on the bed. She had not seen him without a shirt before, and she was pleasantly surprised to see his muscles along his rib cage and his bulging biceps. He had just the right amount of hair on his chest, not bare, but not wooly, and very dark forest under his armpits. She tried not to stare or be nervous, like it was perfectly natural to be in bed with a half-naked man.

She handed him the bottle of lotion and said pointing toward her back, "Would you mind?"

"Sure."

She scooted closer with her back to him and let the robe fall down exposing her back but still covering her breast. It was obvious she was naked underneath the robe too. He shook the lotion, poured some into his firm hands, and began gently massaging her shoulders, neck, and upper back, it smelled like brown sugar. He then worked downward toward her hips, gently tugging the robe away from her to go lower and lower.

"That feels so good," she said.

He applied more lotion and ran his slippery fingers around her rib cage toward the front of her body, at the same time he slowly and gently leaned her backwards onto his chest and touched his hands on her breast, stroking gently.

"Is this ok, my love, if you have a problem, just let me know. We can stop at any time you feel uncomfortable, we will go slow, I have eternity to learn to love you," he said.

"Eli, I love you, and I want to show you and share that love with you completely." When she said those words she turned and lay down beside him on the bed and pulled him on top of her, their lips met and she felt nothing but love for him. He was gentle with her, and took his time to connect spiritually, kissing her gently, tenderly all over her face, and he entered her. It was more beautiful and passionate than she could have ever imagined. She was so grateful that she had never been with another, and she knew without any doubt that he was her bashert.

The two-halves united in marriage were whole, as one again. She no longer thought of herself as a victim, but now as a survivor. This part of her was for her and Eli only; no thoughts allowed intruding upon their intimate moments, ever again. She purged the abusive memories with the fire, and the impurities refined, and love shone through like pure gold. She believed love—like pure gold, is virtually indestructible, it cannot corrode, rust or tarnish, or be destroyed by fire. It is refined and grows purer.

This is what she finally found with Eli, love, trust and intimacy.

# FORTY-ONE

She stood admiring the crashing waves and strength of the ocean. She wondered why they called it 'roaring', it sounded more like hissing followed by a silence: hissing in and draining back to sea and returning unrelenting.

She sensed him behind her before she felt his arms around her and he placed his hands with splayed fingers over her engorged belly. "What are you thinking of, my love?" Eli asked.

She half turned her head while the wind blew her hair wildly, "I'm envisioning our daughter inside me, flopping like a dolphin in this ocean."

With a smile, and kiss on her ear he whispered, "Have I told you how much I love you today?"

"No, you haven't," she turned to face him, resting her swollen belly against him.

"Did you feel her kick?"

"Why do you call her, her, could be him," Eli said.

"I just feel her being in me."

In the last month of their pregnancy, they had taken a 'babymoon', to spend their last days as a couple, anticipating what life as a family of three would be like. They were staying off the east coast of southern Florida, their condominium on the beach to hear and smell the sea in all its vastness. It helped calm her and put her current condition in perspective. When the tide washed in and carried out to sea the day's debris, it was like a new birth. Each morning was a fresh landscape, a gift from the creator.

Their child would be a fresh, clean spirit God was gifting them to nurture and fill with the goodness of humankind. If her early life filled with such sorrows, no child should endure, meant this windfall of blessings with Eli and their baby—it was all worth it. For if she had been given a mundane existence without pain and suffering, and that meant she would not find her beloved—Eli, she would not have chosen that life.

She inhaled the smell of sea salt, trying to retain it for future, when you leave the ocean you forget the scent it carries on the wind. It is hard to describe, somewhat sour, some decay from the primordial space between surface and ocean floor. Not quite like the petrichor of dry earth, the musty, barky smell of fresh rain on the dry earth, but it is recognizable, just not describable. The artist in her marveled at the color of the changing waters with the sunshine, from lightest blue-green on top of white sand, to a murky green in deeper water; while the Dead Sea is the lightest aqua, and the Mediterranean sea with its dark ominous and cold blue. How does the sea know what color to paint, it's all the same salt water, she thought.

Thoughts of the sea brought back her wedding and honeymoon. She thought back on all that they had accomplished in their short marriage. Soon after the wedding, she and Eli returned once again to Kentucky, but this time with a purpose.

They used the funds from the land sale to build an

art and interpretive center, on the five acres she had retained. An endowment allowed a full-time art director that would provide art classes and tutoring for local schoolchildren and teens, helping them with training and other programs for children in need. It employed a fulltime counselor for children that needed support, as she needed but never received. She also funded an annual scholarship program for a local high-school art student. As a fundraiser, the center holds annual retreats for budding artist to come to the region for inspiration from the nature and beauty of the land and for workshops. It also allows the local's exposure to visiting artisans. She would be the first artist in residence to kick off the program, and it was a sold out event.

She caught out the corner of her eye Leah and Joseph approaching them on the beach. Leah's giant belly was casting a wide shadow, and she waddled in the sand trying to remain upright, like one of those boppy clowns that you try to knock over, but never can. As she came and stood next to her friends, Joseph stood behind her just like Eli. His arms encircling her expanding belly too.

Leah said, "So little Mama, have we solved the problems of the world, or are we wondering how we're gonna get these tiny people out of us?"

"That does have me a bit worried," JW answered.

Their pregnancy journeys began almost simultaneously as Leah had been trying to conceive for a year before the wedding. JW realized after her announcement that's why she had stopped drinking wine and began nesting early on. They figured the relaxing waters of the Dead Sea, or the vacation to Israel had worked for both of them, and their due dates were days apart.

Eli had kept his promise to love her through her trauma with his patience and gentleness. She had never known such intimacy, and the fears and pain of the past melted away in his strong and loving embrace. He was all that she needed or wanted, and together they had come together to make new life. They decided they would name their daughter Sarah, after both of their mother's and for faithfulness to God. Leah and Joseph chose to name their son Isaac. Together they would raise their children and share a family and a love like one she had never known.

Standing looking at the ocean, she surmised people are like the sea, ever changing but the same, just water. Whether you boil it, or ice it, whether it is crashing waves or still as a mountain lake cove, some with salt, and some pure and fresh, it is still just water. It is not the water that changes; it is the environment and the pressure and actions upon the water that make it what it is. These waters are changing constantly over eons, but one thing rings true in the end we are the water of one ocean, one creator.

# The End